Tinyburg Tales

Tinyburg Tales

Robert J. Hastings

BROADMAN PRESS
Nashville, Tennessee

Dedicated to my wife, Bessie,
who's been to Tinyburg with me many times

PS3558.A727 T57 1983
Hastings, Robert J.
Tinyburg tales

© Copyright 1983 • Broadman Press
All rights reserved

4252-18
ISBN: 0-8054-5218-4

Dewey Decimal Classification: SC
Subject heading(s): SHORT STORIES / / CHRISTIAN LIFE—FICTION
Library of Congress Catalog Card Number: 83-71167
Printed in the United States of America

ACKNOWLEDGMENTS

Grateful acknowledgment for permission to quote material from other publications is extended to the following: Nazarene Publishing House for "All That Thrills My Soul" by Thoro Harris, Copyright 1931. Renewal 1959 by Nazarene Publishing House. Used by permission. Louis J. Khoury, Cayman Music, Ltd., and Dovan Music, Inc. for "I Can See Clearly Now" by Johnny Nash, © 1972 by Cayman Music, Ltd., used by permission of attorney Louis J. Khoury, whose office administrates the publishing catalog of Dovan Music, Inc. Macmillan Publishing Co. for "In Memory of a Child" by Vachel Lindsay, reprinted with permission of Macmillan Publishing Co. from *Collected Poems* by Vachel Lindsay. Copyright 1914 by Macmillan Publishing Co., renewed 1942 by Elizabeth C. Lindsay. Rodeheaver, Hall-Mack (Subsidiary of Word Music) for "Will the Circle Be Unbroken?" by Ada R. Habershon, Renewal 1935 by Rodeheaver, Hall-Mack Co., and for "Win Them One by One" by C. Austin Miles, Renewal 1943 by the Rodeheaver, Hall-Mack Co. Used by permission. *The Illinois Baptist* and Robert J. Hastings for the minister's prayer in "A Thanksgiving to Remember," often reprinted (including the November 25, 1981, issue of *The Illinois Baptist;* the excerpt from "The Station" from the January 2, 1980, issue of *The Illinois*

Contents

Introduction

It's a place where you know everyone, yet still get along. It's where the men are strong, the women good-looking, and all the children above average. It's a place which, when you visit, you feel like you're twelve years old again. It's always there, yet never there. It's a place where every problem has a happy ending. It's a spot we want to hold on to, come what may. It's Tinyburg, thirty-five miles from Bigtown and the nearest interstate highway and just seven miles south of Pretense. Easy to find, hard to leave. Elusive. Receding into yesterday. Too precious to give up, too good to be true.

In the summer of 1979, searching for a lighter vein in which to couch my editorials for *The Illinois Baptist* newspaper, I created the fictional town of Tinyburg. One by one the residents sprang to life—Clay Barker, Miss Grace, Uncle Billy Cutrell, Aunt Sarah Biggs, "Six-Percent" Hardy, and others. This book is a collection of some of the best of those stories.

Readers, in large numbers, were complimentary. When a reader in the Chicago area praised my stories, I said, "I thought only residents of small towns would enjoy them." He replied, "There's a little of the small town in all of us."

I grew up in Marion, a small town (population then of

9,000) in southern Illinois. It's the only parental home I
ever knew. Mom and Dad spent all their married lives
there and lived in one and the same house almost forty
years. I cried like a homeless baby the day they moved,
although I was nearly thirty-five years old at the time.

I remember the neighborhood grocery store where we
bought Whistle (an orange soft drink) for a nickel a
bottle, the schools, the streets where I rode my bicycle,
the fairgrounds that each September changed magically
into a maze of colored lights and spinning Ferris wheels,
the family garden, the neighbors you knew would be
there every morning when you got up.

Those memoirs I described in an earlier book, *A
Nickel's Worth of Skim Milk: A Boy's View of the Great
Depression* (Carbondale, IL: Southern Illinois Univer-
sity Graphics, 1972).

But Tinyburg is not Marion. For one thing, Tinyburg,
with a population of only 1,873, isn't big enough. Tinyburg is a cameo of many small communities I've visited,
primarily in southern Illinois, western Kentucky, and
middle Tennessee. And, of course, it's fiction.

About the time I began this series, I joined the
National Association for the Preservation and Perpetua-
tion of Storytelling (NAPPS). Membership includes *The
Yarnspinner*, a monthly newsletter. I learned there is a
revival of old-fashioned storytelling throughout America.
Perhaps this is a reaction to television and other electronic entertainment which, though professional, lacks
the intimacy of storytelling.

Thus encouraged, I started telling, as well as writing,
my stories and reaped a double bonus. First, the pleasure of doing so. And second, the "inspiration of the
moment" which helped me improve my plots, add color to

the dialogues, and strengthen the characters.

I've since told these stories in Sunday evening church services, seminary classrooms, dinner meetings, Christmas parties, banquets, nursing homes, senior-adult conferences, and writers' workshops.

Three pieces of literature, long buried in my subconscious, also fed my imagination. The first is a book by Ian Maclaren, *Beside the Bonnie Brier Bush* (Chicago: Donohue, Henneberry & Co., no date). It's a collection of delightful stories about village life in nineteenth-century Scotland.

Second is Thornton Wilder's Pulitzer prizewinning play *Our Town* based on Grover's Corners, New Hampshire. Written in 1938, it makes you want to hold on to today, lest the busy world rob you of life's everyday pleasures.

Third is the book *Heaven in My Hand* by Alice Lee Humphreys (Richmond: John Knox Press, 1950). Alice shares her bittersweet memories of many years as a first-grade teacher in a small town. It always brings a lump to my throat.

I hope I never outlive my love for the people of America who live in small towns. They have a special place in my heart. And there are many of them. According to the 1970 US Census, there were 18,467 towns and villages in the United States with a population of 10,000 or less.

And now, go with me to Tinyburg and let me introduce you to some of the wonderful folks who live there.

ROBERT J. HASTINGS

Another Piece
of Cherry Cobbler

Each fall, Tinyburg Church honors its new members
with a dinner. Seated at the head table with the
Preacher, each gave a testimony on "the kind of member
I hope to be." This fall, places were set for thirty-six new
members, crowding the available space.

Burt David, a securities salesman who'd just retired
from Bigtown, was one of the thirty-six. Arriving early,
Burt chose a seat next to the Preacher. Exuding confi-
dence and dominating every conversation, he was never
at a loss for words. He was a careful dresser; his black,
piercing eyes and bushy eyebrows were in sharp contrast
to his white hair.

Soon after he was served, Burt spotted a business
prospect across the room. Although retired, Burt still
sold investments a day or two a week. So he waved at the
prospect to join him at the head table, since only thirty-
five of the thirty-six new members had shown up. Using
the paper table covering for a writing pad, Burt quickly
scribbled the price earnings ratio of a stock he was
recommending.

Burt also joked with the serving ladies, calling each
one "Sweetheart" or "Honey." He knew this was a proven
way to get plenty of hot coffee, plus an extra serving of

the homemade cherry cobbler he'd spotted in the kitchen.

About time for dessert, Jimmie S., the thirty-sixth new member, walked in. Jimmie, a dishwasher at the Tinyburg Nursing Home, was habitually late for everything. Even on Sundays, the worship service began long before he finished his breakfast dishes. His favorite seat—actually the only place he would sit—was in the middle of the second pew, right in front of the pulpit.

Regular members, knowing his habit, left room near the aisle for him to enter. But if a visitor chanced to sit there, Jimmie climbed right over him, whether it was during a prayer, the offertory, or whatever.

When the Preacher baptized Jimmie, a few members questioned if he knew enough to make a confession. Some said he was mentally retarded, while others concluded he was just a slow learner.

Jimmie was best known for his bright smile. His face seemed to glow, whether washing dishes or sharing a hymnal with a visitor.

But back to the dinner. Because Jimmie was late and Burt David had already given his seat to a business prospect, Jimmie sat at a makeshift table near the back of the church dining room. Since all the cherry cobbler was gone, someone opened him a can of cling peaches and a box of vanilla wafers.

When time came for the testimonies, Burt David was the first on his feet. "This church is a real challenge to me as a new member," he began. "Take the deacons here, who're in middle management. I can help with their goals, priorities, and budgeting. With the right efficiency studies, we can revolutionize our little church."

"I could write job descriptions for members who hold offices," he continued. "Also, I can do time and motion studies for the church secretary, custodian, maybe the pastor. . . . "

The Preacher shifted uneasily. The part-time secretary, who worked only Tuesday and Friday afternoons, covered her mouth as if to stifle a yawn. Only the most observant knew it was a gasp.

Jimmie was the last to speak. The Preacher had to coax him to the front. Visibly embarrassed, Jimmie's usual smile went into hiding. "Just say what's on your heart," whispered the Preacher, reassuring him as best he could.

Jimmie, his hands in his pockets, swallowed hard and looked at the ceiling. "Well," he began slowly, measuring each word, "it's a real purty day and . . . and . . "

"Go on," encouraged the Preacher.

"And . . . well, I shore do love Jesus." And with that, his old smile broke through, like sunlight after a June rain shower. Whereas Burt had gotten polite applause, there was now a strange silence, punctuated by an occasional sniffle or clearing of the throat.

The Preacher was crawling into bed when the phone rang. "It's Fred Turner here," began the late caller. "You've been after me a long time to teach a Bible class, but I kept saying I couldn't talk on my feet. Well, Jimmie got to me tonight. If he can stand up there and say he loves Jesus, I can make a stab at those lessons."

"Fred, that's good news," the Preacher replied. "And you can start Sunday. The only thing, we're out of teachers' helps. But if you'll hold on, I can read you the Bible lesson over the phone."

In a matter of seconds, the Preacher was reading:

> For if there come unto your assembly a man with a
> gold ring, in goodly apparel, and there come in also a
> poor man in vile raiment;
> And ye have respect to him that weareth the gay
> clothing, and say unto him, Sit thou here in a good
> place; and say to the poor, Stand thou there, or sit here
> under my footstool:
> Are ye not then partial . . . and are become judges?
> . . . Hath not God chosen the poor of this world rich in
> faith? (Jas. 2:2-5).

Burt never did get around to writing his job descriptions. Seems most members already knew how to do
more than they were doing.

But the next time you have some extra savings to
invest, you might drive over to Tinyburg and talk to
Burt. It's not far over there—just seven miles south of
Pretense. And while you're there, stop by the nursing
home. If cherry cobbler's on the menu that day, Jimmie
will probably have a piece saved back for you.

If not, he'll still open you a can of peaches!

Myrtle's Pew

There was a crisis in Tinyburg Church—one that threatened its very existence. It all started when the church voted to erect a new educational wing, but to keep and renovate the old sanctuary. The face-lifting would include new pews, carpeting, and lighting. Everyone agreed this was a good idea, for it would mean keeping the ornate woodwork and the Tiffany stained-glass windows, items that couldn't be replaced.

What caused the problem was the pews. The plans were to order custom-made pews to match the curved backs and the distinctive hand carving on the ends of the old ones. But when the trustees learned the price of custom-made pews, the church voted to refinish the old ones.

First, they would be stripped and sanded to remove all the nicks and scratches, then given three coats of clear varnish. To satisfy those who had hoped for new, padded pews, Mr. and Mrs. Clay Barker offered to donate pew cushions. These would be in memory of Mrs. Barker's mother, a longtime Sunday School teacher.

The color selection committee decided to sand and strip one pew as a sample, so everyone could see exactly how it would look. But when the sample was finished, the original wood was much lighter than anyone had imagined. Through the years, coats and coats of varnish and stain, plus the aging of time, had given them a dark mahogany—almost blacklike—finish.

That's what aggravated the problem. Some members wanted to stain the pews back to the deep, dark mahogany they were accustomed to. Others insisted on clear varnish, to bring out the original grain of the wood.

Would you believe the congregation was almost equally divided? Half wanted light pews, half wanted dark. So a special meeting was set to decide the question once and for all.

When the Preacher walked in and saw wall-to-wall people (some who hadn't been in church for years), he'd have settled for folding chairs!

"Now before we vote," the Preacher began, "we want to give everyone an opportunity to express himself. We don't want anyone going home, saying he didn't have a say."

Tugging at his sleeves and tucking them in with his elastic arm bands, Uncle Billy Cutrell was the first to his feet. "I just want everybody here to know that I'll not vote one way or another," he explained. "I think these pews are good enough the way they are. Too much modernizin' going on around here, anyway.

"To be honest, I haven't gotten over the decision a few years back to take out the amen corner. I know several of the older menfolk who've never felt right about it.

"And another thing, we didn't need this new carpet. I remember when mothers used to bring their babies right in the services and made pallets on the floor for the little ones. I think those little tykes got as much out of church back then as they do today in fancy nurseries singing those little patty-cake songs.

"Why, one of the finest protracted meetings we ever saw, mothers had babies lying all over the place, under the pews, some cryin' and some asleep, and some a-playin' with their purties. But nobody cared.

"Today, we need shiny new pews, wall-to-wall carpet, and even soft cushions to sit on. We're gettin' too comfortable—no wonder so many of our folks go to sleep during services.

"'Course I know my vote won't make no difference, but I'm not votin' either way and just wanted all of you to know."

As Uncle Billy sat down, Mrs. Clay Barker let out one of her long, slow sighs that could be heard all the way to the back.

"Anybody else got a word?" asked the Preacher apprehensively, with a "hope-you-don't" tone.

"Yes, I do" spoke up Clay Barker, turning so everyone could see him.

Right here I'd better stop and tell you about Clay. As longtime president of the Tinyburg Realty Company, he's known all over the county. Not only does he buy and sell real estate, but he also conducts auctions, does appraisals, and writes insurance.

Clay Barker's the only man in Tinyburg who wears a coat and tie, 365 days in the year. If you see him at the July 4 picnic, he'll be as dressed up as when he's in his office on Main Street.

He always wears a celluloid penholder in his breast pocket, with a dozen or so ball-point, fountain, and felt-tip pens of assorted sizes and colors. "In my business, you never know when you're gonna close a deal," he often explained. "I dress for business, not play. I believe in getting a fellow on the dotted line while he's in the notion."

Tonight, Clay was wearing his usual array of pens as well as a six-diamond, massive, gold wedding band. He'd never have bought that expensive a ring himself, but he picked this one up for a little nothing at an estate sale.

He did buy, at retail, a matching diamond stick pin for his tie, which he wore only on special occasions. As Clay rose to speak, the Preacher noticed with added trepidation that tonight he had on the stick pin, too. By now, the Preacher sure enough would have settled for folding chairs.

Anyway, Clay Barker cleared his throat, fingered his stick pin, and nervously reached for a black fountain pen which he used as a minipointer to emphasize his point.

"Now dear brothers—and sisters—you can vote anyway your little hearts please. But Mrs. Barker and I just want you to know that if you decide on light pews, there'll be no cushions. We've already selected a color to go with mahogany.

"Besides, Mrs. Barker and I assumed the pews would look like they've always looked. But if you're going to change your minds every day or so, and be wishy washy, then we'll just forget the cushions. In my business, a deal's a deal. I never fool with a customer who can't make up his mind. A long time ago, my daddy said it's not good business to go around lickin' a calf twice. Neither is it good religion."

So back and forth the debate went. It was evident the vote would be close. Then, just as someone was calling for a secret ballot, Myrtle Eagleton raised her hand to speak.

Myrtle, seventy-seven, was sitting in a wheelchair in the aisle back of the last row of pews on the south side. Since suffering a stroke, she felt more comfortable in her wheelchair than a pew.

That night she was wearing a green and white polka-dot dress, trimmed with white cuffs and collar.

When the Preacher recognized her, Myrtle wheeled herself down the aisle, turned, and spoke almost in a whisper. Everyone strained to hear.

"As you know," she began, "I can't come to services like I once did. But if I had my health back, I'd be willing to sit on the floor.

"Do you remember our pastor's sermon two Sundays ago, when he said the Christian life's not so much sitting and listening as it is going and doing? If you ask me, we've got our priorities mixed up.

"In a way, I'm like Uncle Billy here. I'd just as soon leave the pews as they are, for when you sand them down, you're going to erase fifty years of memories. I reared my family in this church, and all over these pews you'll find little scuff marks and scratches left by their shoes.

"That's especially true of that last pew on the left. When I was a teenager and dating Ed, the boy I later married, we often sat on that pew. That's where Ed first held my hand, one Sunday night during the benediction when no one was looking. I was scared to death Daddy would see us.

"Soon after, Ed took his pocketknife and carved our initials on the seat. Talk about the fear of God! If Daddy had seen that, it would have been the absolute end. But he never did, or if so didn't recognize our initials.

"Well, last June," Myrtle continued, her voice now even lower, "we had my husband's funeral here. It was a lovely service. After we got home from the cemetery, I asked my children to drive me back down here to the church. They didn't want to, said I was being too emotional. But I knew what I wanted.

"I came in here alone—it was sundown, and the late June sunlight was streaming through these windows. I eased myself out of my chair into that pew back there, then ran my fingers across those initials. And for a few minutes, I was sixteen years old again!

"So you see why I can't get as excited as some of you about one color or another."

A long, embarrassing silence followed. Lots of handkerchiefs and facial tissues came out of purses and pockets. Then Clay Barker spoke:

"Folks, I think Myrtle has helped us see ourselves as we really are. Proud, yes, and a little childish. I, too, remember the Preacher's sermon on the difference in sitting and serving. So Mrs. Barker and I have just agreed that however you vote, the pew cushions are still on order! And we don't care if they're made out of orange velvet, and you paint the pews bright purple!"

"Aaaaaamen!" shouted Uncle Billy, as if he couldn't wait until the cushions arrived.

"Just a minute, Uncle Billy," Clay interrupted. "I'm not through. I just hate like the dickens to see us vote on this, maybe split the church, upset a lot of folks over a little paint job. So I make a motion, if it's in order, that the Preacher's little boy, Mark, come down here and draw straws and decide it that way."

And so it was.

I was a visitor, and the meeting had gone overtime, so I felt I couldn't stay any longer. So really, I don't know which color they decided on.

I do know that as I walked down the street, I heard the closing hymn, wafting through the open windows. They chose "Just a Closer Walk with Thee." I thought it was fitting, since the Christian walk means more than all the church pews in the world.

So if you want to know the color they decided on, you'll have to visit Tinyburg. If you can't go for a Sunday, stop anytime at Uncle Billy's who lives across the street. He has a key and would be thrilled to unlock the church for you.

And when you go, be sure to sit down for a minute or two in the back pew on the left. (Now that's on the Preacher's left, facing the congregation. It'll be the south side, in case you get mixed up.)

That's the one they call "Myrtle's pew." The reason is that when they did the refinishing, they left hers just like it was—initials and all.

While you're sitting there, run your fingers across the initials and see if you, too, don't feel like you're sixteen again!

Skydivin' for Jesus

Thursday afternoon, right on schedule, the big tractor trailer pulled onto the parking lot of Tinyburg Church, groaning under its load of snow-cone and cotton-candy machines, costume changes, cartons of books, souvenirs, and sound systems. The slogan, painted in big, red letters on the side, caught the eye of everyone: "Skydivin' for Jesus."

Other vehicles, such as campers, sound trucks, pickups, and cars pulled in alongside.

"Say, I wasn't expectin' Coxey's Army," beamed the Preacher as he greeted Ted Albright, a tall, lanky fellow wearing cowboy hat and boots.

"Well, to draw the kind of crowd we promised in our contract, you've got to pull out all the stops," Ted explained, rubbing the long sideburns that reached almost to his jaws. "Remember, when I jump out of that plane tomorrow and fall 500 feet before I yank that cord, you can rest assured I'll thrill everyone in Tinyburg, young and old alike."

"And to hold the crowd between jumps, we brought along some concessions, such as pony rides, guess-your-weight experts, and cotton candy," Ted continued as he adjusted his belt, fastened with the biggest rhinestone buckle the Preacher had ever seen.

"'Course we'll need some hookups, you know—tap into your church's water, sewer, and electric," Ted continued. "And some signs directing folks to your rest rooms. And while you're at it, you'd better lay in more paper towels, cups, and the like, for you're gonna see the biggest turnout this weekend in the history of your church. To really thrill folks, you've gotta think big, plan big, even spend big!"

About that time Billy Cutrell, who lived across the street from the church, ambled over, little question marks dancing in his eyes. Although most folks called him "Uncle Billy Told-You-So," he was satisfied today just to wear a knowing look and, for the time being, to say nothing.

It took almost all day Friday to do the hookups, stake out the pony rides, and set up the stands. By noon a maze of electric wires snaked all over the lawn, from nearly every wall plug in the church. Ted also painted a big circle, or bull's-eye, in the center of the parking lot.

"That's awfully bright paint," the Preacher opined. "Think we can ever clean it up?"

"Look, Preacher, when you're up there 3,000 to 4,000 feet in the air, jumpin' out of a plane, you want a target you can see. That's why we use this yellow striping paint, the same kind the highway department buys. What if it doesn't wash off? The kids can play games out here all summer, using the bull's-eye for home base or whatever."

The plan was simple: On Saturday, Joe would parachute from a small plane at 10:00, 2:00, and 4:30, guaranteeing to land inside the circle two out of the three times. Each time, he would give his testimony, "Skydiving for Jesus is better than high living for Satan." On Sunday, he would stay over to autograph his book, *On Target with*

Ted. Also, wearing his jump suit, he would pose with the youngsters in the yellow circle for photographs. The Preacher would be in the pulpit bringing a message on the topic "Look Before You Leap," using sermon ideas furnished by Ted. The youth choir would sing a musical jingle which Ted himself had written and copyrighted:

> Never jump without aiming;
> Never aim without jumping;
> Those who fear will never jump,
> Those who wait will never score.

True, the Preacher felt a tingle of apprehension. But the whole setup looked so nice that he went to bed Friday night confident that Saturday and Sunday would be the biggest weekend in the church's history. Then there was the 1 percent commission on all sales, which would be coming to the church. Too, he kept reciting Ted's promise, "Preacher, it just thrills me to death to be in Tinyburg and help your church."

Saturday morning his phone rang at 6:00. "Preacher, I hate like the dickens to get you outta bed so early," apologized the custodian. "But Ted just turned on all these motors and lights and loud speakers. And when he did, he blew every fuse in the church. A big blue flame shot out from the fuse box, and if I hadn't been there, the whole church would probably have burnt down. And now we're outta' power. What are we gonna do?"

"There's no repair service open on Saturday," he continued. "And if we call Bigtown Electric Company, it'll cost a fortune for them to make a service call out here on a weekend."

"Go ahead and call Bigtown," the Preacher ordered. "After all, we've got our 1 percent commission to look forward to."

As Ted predicted, huge crowds turned out. It was a bright, still day, with little wind, and he landed in the bull's eye all three times. The townspeople spent freely between the jumps, and by nightfall the grounds were littered with paper cups, soft drink bottles, bursted balloons, and candy wrappers. But so what? Never had so many turned out for a church event, and never had so many promised to attend Sunday services. "Maybe I *haven't* been thinking big enough," the Preacher told himself as he dozed off to sleep.

Sunday morning, the Preacher's clock radio had just come on to "I'm a Rhinestone Cowboy" by a country singer, when the custodian called again.

"Preacher, I hate like the dickens to call you this time of morning, but . . . "

For a fleeting moment, the Preacher wished it were Monday.

" . . . but the thing is, well, you know all those folks using our bath rooms yesterday, and all those camper hookups . . . "

"Yes, go on . . . "

"Well, we got sewer water backed up all over the church lawn, and it's starting to run in one of the basement windows, and I don't know who . . . "

By now, the Preacher was unashamedly wishing for Monday.

It was just a short walk over to the church, but it took the Preacher long enough to decide he'd had all the skydiving for Jesus he wanted. Although the diving crew was still asleep, the Preacher knocked boldly on Ted's camper.

"Ted, I know we agreed for you to stay over until Sunday noon to autograph your books and help draw a

crowd. And my watch says it's only 6:00 AM, but my
heart tells me it's noon. So I'd be obliged if you and your
crew would get all your paraphernalia off our lot in
exactly one hour."

Rubbing his eyes in disbelief, Ted replied, "Why,
Preacher, I've been to grand openings, anniversaries,
homecomings, reunions, July 4 picnics, ribbon cuttings,
you name it. But this is the first time anyone's ever asked
little ole Ted to just pick up and move on. We got another
thrillin' morning ahead of us.

"And just think of all those little old kiddoes who'll be
disappointed when I'm not here to autograph their
books," he continued, fastening his rhinestone belt
buckle. "I was even gonna wear my diving outfit again
and let anyone get their pictures took, standin' beside
me, whether they buy a book or not . . . "

"Ted," the Preacher said, lowering his voice, "there's
nothing wrong with you. You've kept your bargain. I
believe your testimony.

"It's true we ought to hit the bull's-eye for Jesus. And
you've already helped our church, just getting us together for a good time.

"But it's me that's wrong. I got my priorities mixed up.
And I know it's wrong to break a contract. But if you'll
move out, we'll forget our one percent commission."

As the last camper disappeared around the corner, led
by the "Skydivin' for Jesus" trailer, Uncle Billy came out
his front door in a frayed, blue bathrobe looking for his
Sunday paper. "Hi, Preacher," he waved across the
street. "I told you those show people never keep their
word." The Preacher wanted to tell Billy the truth, but
the words froze in his throat.

At the eleven o'clock service, the Preacher took full

responsibility for Ted's absence. "I don't feel like preaching," he continued. "Actually, I've already been preached to myself. I've majored too much on thrilling folks, not filling them. So since we're all tired, anyway, and have a lot of cleaning up to do, I'll just read a short Scripture."

> Then was Jesus led up of the Spirit into the wilderness to be tempted of the devil. . . . Then the devil taketh him up into the holy city, and setteth him on a pinnacle of the temple,
> And saith unto him, If thou be the Son of God, cast thyself down: for it is written, He shall give his angels charge concerning thee: and in their hands they shall bear thee up, lest at any time thou dash thy foot against a stone.
> Jesus said unto him, It is written again, Thou shalt not tempt the Lord thy God (Matt. 4:1,5-7).

Following the Scripture reading, the Preacher asked the congregation to turn to page 369 in their hymnals.

"All around us, folks are looking for thrills," he explained. "And our churches face the same temptation that Jesus did long ago, to put on a sideshow to draw a crowd. Frankly, I'd rather have fewer churchgoers, and to know they were thrilled by the gospel, and not by gaudiness. If you can sing it with meaning, join with me now in singing the chorus:

> All that thrills my soul is Jesus,
> He is more than life to me;
> And the fairest of ten thousand
> In my blessed Lord I see.

THORO HARRIS

Dear reader, if you find this story hard to believe, I

don't guess I can blame you. I do suggest that the next time you're in Tinyburg, you stop by the church parking lot. Although it's faded with time, you can still make out that bull's-eye, made with bright orange paint. And in the church library, you can still check out a copy of the skydiver's book, *On Target with Ted*.

Then you can draw your own conclusion!

A Wedding

Architecturally speaking, the Tinyburg Church is a wedding of the modern and traditional.

A new educational unit, complete with the latest teaching aids, was dedicated just five years ago. The white, frame sanctuary has stood there longer than most folks can remember. An all-weather, covered walkway joins the two, as if in matrimony.

The sanctuary itself—topped by a steeple, with its arched windows of stained glass and furnished with three sections of old-fashioned, curved pews—is truly a picture-book setting.

The organ is old but mellow. The stained glass is hard to clean but exquisite in the morning and evening sunlight. The pendulum clock to the right of the pulpit never did keep time, but it does evoke a timelessness that speaks of the agelessness of God.

The dark-mahogany, paneled woodwork that outlines the doors and windows and wraps itself around the choir and pulpit area gives off a faint aroma of furniture polish, the residue of hundreds of dusting cloths over the years.

The richly carved ends of the curved pews speak of a day when labor was cheaper, and beauty was loved for beauty's sake.

Two or three times in living memory someone has

proposed tearing down the old sanctuary in favor of one
with such conveniences as ground-level entrances. But
sentiment has prevailed, and the traditional house of
worship still stands at the corner of North Garfield and
East Logan.

Many of the old-timers can recall when all the classes
met in the auditorium and basement, before the educational building was completed. Back then, a pupil could
sit in one class and hear the lesson explained by at least
three other teachers in nearby pews. So if one didn't like
one teacher, he could still look interested but concentrate
on what another was saying. In fact, he could rotate his
attention, Sunday by Sunday, to first this teacher and
then that one.

It was probably thirty years ago that the church
invited a specialist to lead them in a Sunday School
enlargement campaign.

"The very first step is to curtain off the auditorium, so
the classes will be separated," he advised. "At least you
won't see the other pupils, even if you do hear them."

So the ladies brought their sewing machines and
whipped up yards of unbleached muslin into curtains. In
fact, the Tinyburg Dry Goods Store soon ran out and had
to send a rush order to Bigtown for more. "We never sell
this much unbleached muslin in a year," the clerk sighed.

Once the ladies sewed the curtains to brass drapery
rings, they threaded them onto clothesline wires. The
men then strung the wires, replete with flowing muslin,
making twelve curtained classrooms. Two lines went
down the aisles, plus three lines from side to side. Using
turnbuckles and metal eye screws, they pulled and
strained to make the lines taut. "Pull harder, or they'll

sag and drag the floor," the visiting specialist warned
from his command post in the pulpit.

When one of the eye screws accidentally pulled away
from the wall, that wire recoiled with such force that the
whole section of curtains, wires, turnbuckles, and drapery rings rolled itself into a bundle like a giant snowball.
It took more time to unravel and put it back in place than
it did to string the whole job.

"I hope those wires are up there for good," observed
Uncle Billy Told-You-So, "for if you ever take all of them
down at one time, you're in for one big mess. You could
never sort out those wires and other apparatus."

"Now don't get excited," the Preacher cautioned.
"Those curtains are there to stay until we get our new
educational building."

Most of the teachers and pupils were pleased with the
new arrangement. However, since the pews had curved
backs, each pew now showed up in at least two classes.
The guest specialist had not anticipated this, since in
other churches he'd helped the pews were straight.

Six months later, Mr. and Mrs. Clay Barker announced
the engagement of their only daughter, Candice, who
was just finishing her freshman year in college.

From childhood, Candice had been outgoing and
friendly like her dad. She was always giving little
recitations and readings, and usually had a part in the
Easter and Christmas plays. In high school she was a
cheerleader and held leading roles in the junior and
senior plays. She liked nothing better than to read the
movie magazines down at the Tinyburg Pharmacy and
dream of the day when her name would appear in bright
lights—maybe on Broadway!

At the state university, she started out to major in theater, but when Candice was growing up, few women dreamed of both marriage and a career. So when Ted Carpenter, her high-school sweetheart, kept writing her letters from back home, saying he would go stark raving mad if she didn't marry him, romance conquered the stage, and the actress settled down in Tinyburg to be a housewife.

But although she was giving up the stage as a career, she was determined that her wedding should be as dramatic and theatrical as good taste allowed. Some folks, awed by the preparations, noted that she had more bridesmaids than most brides have as wedding guests.

When Candice and Ted sat down with the Preacher to go over the plans, Candice confessed her one big worry.

"It's those hideous Sunday School curtains and those clotheslines stretched all across the church," she began. "I've always dreamed of a beautiful church wedding, but all those billowing curtains make it look like a Chinese laundry. And even if you pin the curtains against the walls, they'll still hide the candles in the windowsills— maybe even catch on fire.

"Preacher, it's just no fit setting for a wedding, and Ted and I wonder if we could take all the curtains down, just for that one night?"

The Preacher, surprised at such a request, squirmed and looked at the ceiling. "Candice, do you know what will happen to all that wire and curtains if we loosen those turnbuckles? I want to be reasonable, but . . . "

"Now, Pastor," she interrupted, "I don't mean to burden anyone. Daddy and Ted will put them back, won't you Teddy? We're honeymooning out at the state park lodge, and Teddy can run back in Saturday afternoon and do it in no time."

And so there was nothing to do but take them down—curtains, drapery rings, turnbuckles, eye screws, and clotheslines. Each immediately rolled itself into an unmanageable bundle, which the custodian piled in a corner of the basement.

The morning of the wedding when the couple came by to sign the marriage certificate, the Preacher's mouth dropped open when he saw Ted with his right arm in a sling. "We went down to buy some traveler's checks and Ted walked right through those new glass doors at the Tinyburg Bank," Candice explained, "and broke his wrist."

Everyone agreed it was one of the loveliest weddings Tinyburg ever witnessed, even if the groom wore a sling. The June weather was warm but pleasant, the flowers wafted a delicate perfume over the congregation, the candles—unobstructed by curtains—flickered joyfully, and the bride was as beautiful as the storybooks say she should be.

But if a groom can't carry his bride across the threshold with a broken wrist, who could expect him to stretch clothesline wires and twist turnbuckles?

So Sunday morning dawned with the curtains still piled in a heap on the basement floor. And without the familiar curtains, no one knew where to sit.

Feeling some responsibility for the mix-up, Clay Barker stood to make an announcement. "Folks, for old times' sake, why don't we just all assemble down here at the front and have one big class? And I nominate Uncle Billy Cutrell to be our teacher."

Before reading the Scripture lesson, Uncle Billy cleared his throat the way he does when making a propitious announcement.

"Now, I know some of us are upset, which is normal when pushed out of our regular meeting place. And I know it's going to be a job to put those curtains back. But I think it was worth it. As I sat on my front porch watching all those wonderful young people coming out from the wedding, laughing and squealing, I thought how great it was that Candice and Ted wanted a church wedding. You know, so many of our young folk keep running off across the state line to get married. But they wanted to marry here, and they wanted it to be pretty, and I can't say I blame them.

"One more thing, if some of you fellows will meet me over here tomorrow night, we'll straighten out these wires one way or another. And don't worry about me breaking my wrist, for I'm not about to walk through any glass doors at the Tinyburg Bank. The day I saw them putting them in, I said to myself, *I'm having nothing to do with a bank where you can look right in and see what everybody's doing,* so I pulled out my little dab of money right then."

"And now for the lesson. No . . . one other thing. This one big class sure looks good to me. Reminds me of an old Sunday School selection we always sang on Rally Day. I know it's not in our new songbooks, but let's all join in and just sing out from our hearts:

> **If you bring the one next to you**
> **And I'll bring the one next to me;**
> **In all kinds of weather**
> **We'll all work together,**
> **And see what can be done.**

So, you bring the one next to you,
And I'll bring the one next to me;
In no time at all
We'll have them all,
So win them, win them, one by one!

C. Austin Miles

By now the Sunday School bell had rung, and it was time for worship. Even though Uncle Billy never got around to the Bible lesson itself, some of the folks who were there that morning said they learned more than they usually did in their curtained cubicles. Lessons such as love and romance, humor and cooperation, friendship and goodwill.

The Cinnamon Rolls

Mrs. Clay Barker, Aunt Sarah Biggs, and Mrs. Earl (Opal) Baggett were on a committee to plan the annual church homecoming. "This year, let's honor the pastors' wives who've served us through the years," Aunt Sarah suggested, and her idea was unanimously adopted.

(Mr. Barker is president of Tinyburg Realty. Aunt Sarah is Tinyburg's "defender of the faith." Mr. Baggett, retired, frames pictures as a hobby).

Plans included a small booklet, with photos and biographical sketches of pastors' wives over the past fifty years. On a given morning, the committee met with Opal to select the contents. While waiting to start their meeting, the ladies fell into a discussion of who'd been their favorites.

"It won't take me long to tell which I liked best," volunteered Aunt Sarah. "My favorite was Martha. Oh, I don't mean any reflection on Carol, our Preacher's wife now. But Martha was a model in so many ways."

"What I mean is, she was such a good housekeeper and cook. We always had the best church suppers when she planned them. And if anyone in the community was sick or in sorrow, she was on their doorstep with one of her famous blackberry cobblers.

41

"And what a housekeeper! She polished her windows until they shone like mirrors. Never a dirty dish laying around, either. And her children the same way. Hair always combed, very neat, not falling down in their eyes. When they came to church, each looked as if he'd just come out of a bandbox. They were courteous, too. When you'd call the pastorium, if one of the youngsters answered, it was always 'Yes, Ma'am' and 'Yes, Sir' and 'No Ma'am' and 'No Sir.'"

"That's quite a contrast with our minister's family today. When I called the other day, Andrew, their oldest boy, was playing his records so loud that I couldn't even hear what he mumbled, when he answered."

"I liked Martha too," joined in Mrs. Barker, "but as for a favorite, it's a tie between Rosalyn and Mary Ann. Both were top-notch ministers' wives. Take Marilyn. She could make a piano talk. And sing—like you never heard in your life. Always brought tears to my eyes. And remember how she led our music program? Organized a children's chorus, directed the adult choir, put on the biggest Easter programs ever.

"And Mary Ann, our pastor's wife just before her, you couldn't hardly beat her, either. Of course, in a different way. But she was so efficient. She used to cut the stencils for our church bulletins. Fact is, we never had bulletins until she came. She'd work two or three afternoons a week in the church office—never thought about paying a secretary back then.

"And I understand she typed her husband's sermons, and some even say she wrote them when he got in a bind," Mrs. Barker continued. "And if he ever missed a midweek service, why she could step in and give one of the nicest devotionals you ever heard. Rosalyn and Mary

Ann were two fine women—one in the choir, one in the church office."

Opal Baggett had been strangely silent. "Opal, you've lived in Tinyburg a long time. Which pastor's wife was your favorite?" Aunt Sarah asked.

"Oh, it's hard to say. I loved all of them," she replied. "Of course," joined in the other two ladies, "that's one nice thing about our church—we have a reputation for backing our pastors, encouraging them, loving them. Course that don't keep us from having our favorites."

The three women were sitting around Opal's kitchen table, and as she served some of her homemade cider and hot, fresh doughnuts, she finally admitted that yes, she did have a favorite.

"I guess I'd have to say Carol, our Preacher's wife right now."

"Carol?" Aunt Sarah asked, emphasizing the question mark more than the name itself. "Carol's a sweet girl, but when you compare her with Martha and Rosalyn, she can't hold a candle. In a practical way, I mean. Have you been in her house often? I don't think she knows what a clothes closet is. A pile of clothing in this corner, another pile in that corner. From the way her three boys look when they come to church, each one evidently goes to the pile and picks out whatever's on top.

"Do you remember when Mark, their youngest, was about three years old, and they had a wading pool in the backyard? Well, one afternoon Mark had been splashing around in that pool; when it came time for the midweek service, Carol just dried him off, put a little top on him, and let him come to church in his swimsuit. That was right after Mrs. Barker here had given the pew cushions in memory of her mother. Little Mark plopped right down on one of these new cushions and left a wet ring where he'd sat. Carol didn't say a word of apology. I don't think she even noticed.

"True, Carol's got a heart of gold. But that's not enough, especially for a minister's wife. You've gotta have a little common sense up there in your head, as well as some gold in your heart."

"And another thing about Carol, as much as I love her," joined in Mrs. Barker, "is how she's so, well, undisciplinedlike. For example, last August the little peach trees in our backyard bore three bushels of fruit. I gave one bushel to Carol, thinking she'd can them for winter. Fact is, I went through and picked out the best ones for her—even washed them.

"Well, she'd peeled about half of them the next morning, when the boys started begging her to take them to the amusement park in Bigtown. Said school was about to start, and they wouldn't get another chance. Would you believe she left that half bushel of peeled peaches right there on the kitchen cabinet, packed a lunch, and took those boys to Bigtown? I understood they rode on every ride in the park, didn't get back to Tinyburg until midnight. It was a hot day, and when she got home those peaches had turned dark, some even soured.

"I understand she had to throw out most of them. Made me sick at my stomach. You'd think the Preacher, who stayed home, would have done something with those peaches. But he didn't. And I don't call that much of an example for the younger parents in our congregation."

When both women noticed a hurt look on Opal's face, they quickly apologized for not letting her tell why she preferred Carol.

"It's like this," Opal began. "You ladies remember a

couple of years ago, when we faced a big disappointment in our family? Well, one Monday morning it was raining, and I was blue and felt like the whole world was caving in on me. I had a fresh batch of cinnamon rolls in the oven and on an impulse, called Carol and asked if she wanted to join me for coffee.

"Carol said she'd just put a big basket of clothes in the washer, but they could wait, and she'd be right over.

"Well, I guess I unloaded on her. Right at this table where we're sitting now. I just unburdened myself."

"Did Carol counsel with you and give you some helpful advice?" quizzed Aunt Sarah.

"Not exactly. In fact, she didn't say much of anything. Just sat there and listened. Then she started crying. And then I started. And the more I cried, the more she cried. And the more she cried, the more I cried.

"It just seemed like those tears cleared the air, washed a lot of sorrow out of my heart. Carol didn't offer me any pat answers like 'There's a silver lining in every cloud' or 'The Lord won't send more on us than we can bear.' I'd heard all that. She just listened and cried and listened . . .

"No, she didn't have an answer—but she did give me hope.

"Well, when it came time for Carol to leave, I saw her to the door, and by then the sun had come out. And as she was backing the car out of the drive, a rainbow just materialized and seemed to circle the whole town in its arms. I've never seen an angel driving a car, but as she drove away she sure looked like one to me.

"I came back inside and, from force of habit, turned on the radio. And would you believe that someone was singing:

I can see clearly now
The rain has gone;
I can see all obstacles in my way;
Gone are the dark clouds that had me blind.
It's gonna be a bright, bright, sunshiny day;
It's gonna be a bright, bright, sunshiny day!

JOHNNY NASH

"And ladies, it was! And that's why I vote for Carol!"

Fred's New Baptistry

Baptizing folks at the Tinyburg Church used to be a major undertaking, since the baptistry was concealed under the rostrum.

First you moved the pulpit to one side, then rolled up the carpet and raised the trapdoor. Next you moved in portable screens for the privacy of the candidates. "We need a new baptistry the worst in the world," Mrs. Clay Barker had said so often that she sounded like a tape recording. "Up higher, back of the choir, so we won't have to bring in Coxey's Army to move all this furniture for a baptizing. Besides, those boards are getting old and creaky. Someone's liable to get hurt."

"No," argued Aunt Sarah Biggs. "My mother and grandmother were baptized there; it wouldn't seem right and proper to move it."

But when Clay Barker, who sings bass in the men's quartet, got carried away at the annual homecoming, patting his foot to the rhythm, the trapdoor strained under his weight. If he hadn't grabbed the edge of the pulpit, he'd have fallen in the water for sure.

That decided it. The members voted for a new baptistry.

They gave the job to Fred "Fixit" Turner, president of the Fixit Construction Company. The title was hardly necessary, since Fred was the sole employee. Fred could do anything—plumbing, wiring, carpentry, painting, or whatever.

One morning at the Tinyburg Cafe, where Fred always has breakfast, a friend said, "Fred, I see you've got religion—your truck's parked down by the church every morning."

"Oh, that," answered Fred, an outgoing fellow who often said he gets up on the funny side of the bed. "Didn't you know about the new baptistry?"

Then, lowering his voice in mock solemnity, he whispered, "If you fellows will scoot up close and promise not to tell, I'll let you in on a secret. When the trustees learned what a new baptistry would cost, they told me just to fix up the old one."

"Oh, I'm making a few changes," he grinned, proving the cafe owner's boast that as long as Fred ate breakfast there he didn't need to advertise, since so many customers dropped by to hear his funny stories. "One big change is the hinges. I'm reversing them. Also connecting the trapdoor latch to a long rope which reaches down into the basement."

"You know that long-winded preacher they have? Well, once the baptistry's fixed, one deacon's going to sit on the front row with another stationed under him in the basement. And the first Sunday the preacher goes past twelve o'clock the upstairs deacon will tap on the floor, signaling the basement deacon to yank the rope and dump the preacher into his own baptistry!"

At this, the fellows at his table roared so loud that an old tom cat, asleep on a hot water radiator, jumped up and squealed like a weasel.

On the Tuesday before the Sunday the new baptistry

was to be dedicated, Fred picked up his four-year-old grandson after work and drove out to the city reservoir. After parking the panel truck at the top of a steep incline, they walked out to the edge of a long pier to fish in deep water.

Seeing he'd forgotten his bait, Fred warned the boy to sit still while he went back to the truck. Fred had just reached the top of the hill when he heard a splash. His grandson had fallen in.

Cursing himself for his negligence, Fred ran down the hill, kicking off his boots and jumping in. Although his grandson had disappeared beneath the water, Fred was able to find him with little difficulty.

He seemed OK, except he'd swallowed a lot of muddy water. He was coughing and spitting up so that Fred decided to run him by the emergency room.

En route, the little fellow kept trying to talk. "I wasn't afraid, Gramps, really I wasn't. I knew you'd save me."

The doctor said that aside from being nauseated by all the muddy water he'd swallowed, the boy was fine. Even in the emergency room, the little fellow kept repeating, "I wasn't scared. I knew Gramps would pull me out."

Fred surprised a lot of folks by attending church the following Sunday. "Probably out of respect," observed Uncle Billy Cutrell, "since he got the contract for the new baptistry."

Fred further surprised everyone by making a profession of faith and asking for membership. "If it's not asking too much," he explained, "I'd like to be the first person in that baptistry tonight. Many of you have invited me over the years, but I always put you off with some smart-aleck remark such as 'The roof might cave in.' But that was just my way of putting you off."

"I grew up hearing that the Lord might save you if you plead and cry long enough. I said to myself then that if that's what it takes to be a Christian, I'd skip it. But something changed my mind last Tuesday when my grandson almost drowned. He kept saying he wasn't scared—knew I'd save him.

"I've come to see that the Christian life isn't based on how hard we try, but how much we trust the good Lord to do for us what we can't manage ourselves. So if you can take a new member on that basis, I'm ready."

As the Preacher led Fred into the new baptistry that night, the choir sang softly:

> I was sinking deep in sin,
>   Far from the peaceful shore,
> Very deeply stained within,
>   Sinking to rise no more;
> But the Master of the sea
>   Heard my despairing cry,
> From the waters lifted me,
>   Now safe am I.

JAMES ROWE

Although the old baptistry has long since been covered over with new carpeting, folks in Tinyburg still laugh about Fred's trapdoor.

What they don't laugh about is Fred's religion. It's as real as the rescue of his grandson from the city reservoir, many years ago.

A Curl in a Pig's Tail

"Preacher, what you need is a doctor's degree like me," explained Rev. Henry Moss, D.D., a neighboring pastor in Bigtown.

"But Tinyburg's never had a pastor with a doctor's degree," the Preacher replied, somewhat apologetically. "I don't know how the folks would accept a 'doctor' in the pulpit. And besides, with my growing family, I don't have the time or money to go back to the seminary for graduate work."

"Fiddlesticks," replied Rev. Moss. "The folks at Tinyburg would swell with pride to call you 'doctor.' And as far as going back to school's concerned, you know enough already to pastor a church three times the size of this one. I've got the address of a firm out in California that will give you any kind of degree you want, for just a modest handling fee."

"You mean a mail-order doctorate?" the Preacher asked.

"What's wrong with mail order?" Rev. Moss replied. "Your folks buy everything else by mail—Sears, Ward's, Penney's. Why get upset about ordering a doctor's degree, too?"

In his heart of hearts, the Preacher had secretly wanted a doctor's degree worse than he had longed for a red fire truck on his fifth birthday. The words *reverend doctor* sounded so ecclesiastical. And maybe a title to his name would also lend a new aura of success to his entire personality!

"But suppose I order one of these degrees?" he asked. "Would that guarantee folks calling me 'doctor'?"

"That's no problem," replied Rev. Moss. "Just do like I did. Change all your stationery and church bulletins so 'Dr.' will be in front of your name. When the telephone rings, train your secretary to say, 'Yes, I'll let you talk to Dr. So-and-So,' or 'No, Dr. So-and-so isn't in, but I'll have the doctor call you back.' And when you prepare a release for the *Tinyburg News*, always put doctor in front of your name. You'll be surprised how quickly the folks will catch on."

The Preacher was so proud when he unwrapped his $25 "degree," complete with seal and fancy ribbon. His first thought was to frame it and hang it in his office. But fearing some visitors might know the difference, he decided on his bedroom at home.

That way he could glance at it each morning and, like a cup of strong coffee, it would give him a running start on the new day.

Most of the members went along with the new "honor" given their pastor. The *Tinyburg News* even published his picture and a front-page story. Only Uncle Billy-Told-You-So made an issue out of it. "I've never called anybody 'reverend' or 'doctor' and I'm not about to start now," he said. "I never knew of a curl in a pig's tail that improved the flavor of the bacon."

That fall, as a member of the local school board, the Preacher sat in on a hearing that involved J. C. Wagner, a high school biology teacher. It seems Mr. Wagner, although a bona fide college graduate, had falsified his transcript by adding several postgraduate courses. For three years, he had enjoyed extra pay based on this "study" which now was shown to be false.

It was humiliating for both the board and Mr. Wagner, for one had done the fooling, and the other had been fooled. But the board sensed a genuine penitence in J. C., and the matter was resolved in a manner that was redemptive to all concerned.

The next night, the Preacher kindled the first fire of the season in his fireplace. To start the fire, he removed his oversize "doctorate" from its frame, crumpled it in his hands, and lit it with a match. Then he added the new church stationery.

It was one of the coziest fires he had ever kindled, and he enjoyed its warmth and dancing light as never before.

The Ragpicker

A one-legged ragpicker lived just outside the city limits of Tinyburg. Otherwise, zoning laws would have closed him down long ago. His house—if you could call it that—was made of sheets of corrugated metal roofing and other scrap materials. Some said the dirt floor was covered by odds and ends of old linoleums. Automobile tires, packing crates, tin cans, scrap lumber, and what have you, littered the yard. An emaciated goat served as yardman and source of milk.

The yard was enclosed with odds and ends of fencing which the ragpicker had picked up on his daily rounds. He and his horse-drawn wagon were a familiar sight on the streets of Tinyburg, accompanied by two hungry-looking dogs who scurried here and there, snatching at every available bit of food. "My dogs and my goat look out for themselves," he often said. "I'm not about to haul in special food for them."

For his own food, he depended mainly on half-rotten fruits and soggy vegetables he found in the trash bins at the town's two grocery stores.

Some folks in Tinyburg said he was as surly as his two dogs, which would fight any day over a bone already as clean as the town clerk's bald head. Others said he had a

streak of kindness, buried under the grime of his shape-
less clothing.

Everyone agreed on one thing: he was a hard worker.
Although he used one hand and arm to support himself
on a single crutch, relieving the weight on his left peg
leg, he could sift through junk piles of any size with
amazing speed, using only his right hand.

Years of grubbing in trash and garbage had broken
most of his fingernails back to the quick, and dirt was so
imbedded on his face, neck, and hands that he looked as
if he were covered with blackheads.

One day the Preacher suggested that someone visit
the ragpicker, or at least go with him on a call to his
shack. But no one volunteered. "Why, Preacher, if that
ragpicker came to church, folks wouldn't even go near
him," one member said. "Do you know how rotten
cabbage smells? Would you want one of your kids sitting
next to him, using the same rest rooms, handling the
same hymnbooks? Now if you want some of us to go out
there with a Thanksgiving basket, that's OK. But bringing him right here in the church house is another matter."

The Preacher fished around for a suitable answer; but
for the moment, gave up trying to get the ragpicker's
name on the church's prospect list.

A few nights later, the Preacher had a strange dream.
He dreamed that Jesus Christ was coming to Bigtown,
the state capital, just thirty-five miles from Tinyburg.
Like anyone else who could possibly make the trip, the
pastor drove to Bigtown in time to see the Lord's plane
land at the civic airport.

Long before noon, when the plane was due, the streets
and highways around Bigtown were hopelessly jammed.
Many visitors slept in their cars or in the city parks,

after the motels quickly sold out. Hot dog and souvenir stands sprung up all over the place. The most popular items were prints of Warner Sallman's *Head of Christ* and the Lord's Prayer engraved on half-dollar size medallions.

Plans included a parade, ending at a downtown intersection, where a special platform had been erected. There would be bands and choirs and flags and Boy Scout troops and civic clubs and veterans in the parade, headed by the governor, mayor, and top business and religious leaders. Rumor was that the Lord would deliver "The Sermon on the Mount" from the downtown platform. Many speculated on whether he would use the version of the sermon from the King James Version, *The Living Bible, Today's English Version,* or maybe the American Standard Version.

Uncle Billy Told-You-So contended that if the Lord used anything but the King James Version, he would leave, right in the middle of the sermon, even if he was lucky enough to be sitting right down in front.

"I'm not listenin' to nothin' but the pure Bible, just like King James' secretaries took it down," Uncle Billy affirmed.

The Preacher edged his way to the airport, where he could get a good view of the incoming plane and the welcoming party. Right on time, the celestial plane landed, and Jesus appeared at the door. Now all was in readiness for the parade. However, at the last minute, a dispute arose over who was to ride in the limousine with Christ. Presumably, details were all arranged as to who should ride in the front car, the second car, and so on.

By the time the argument was settled, Jesus was nowhere to be found. He seemed to have melted in the crowd. Near pandemonium broke out. "Frauds!" cried some hecklers. "We knew it was a gimmick. Jesus Christ's not coming to Bigtown. Just a big promotional deal to sell souvenirs and benefit the motels."

Others, silent, were crushed with broken hopes. Slowly, the crowd dispersed, and it was long past dark before the highways were cleared of all congestion.

In his dream, the Preacher now made his way back to Tinyburg, arriving on the outskirts of town about 10:00 PM. It was a bright, moonlit night, and as he passed the ragpicker's shack, he thought he could make out two figures sitting on the doorstep. This was odd, since the ragpicker had no known friends. (A few years ago, a distant relative of the ragpicker had stopped by the Tinyburg Funeral Home and prepaid for a simple burial. "When he dies, don't call us," he had said. "Bury him the same day and forget the marker, for no one'll ever be looking for his grave.")

The Preacher braked his car to a sudden stop, got out, walked up to the gateless fence, and stepped over it. To his surprise, the second person was the Lord! And surprise of surprises, his arms were around the ragpicker's shoulders.

The Preacher then noted that the Lord was speaking softly into the ragpicker's ear. Edging closer, he listened closely, and what he overheard was what the curiosity seekers in Bigtown had failed to hear:

> Blessed are the poor in spirit: for theirs is the kingdom of heaven.
> Blessed are they that mourn: for they shall be comforted.
> Blessed are the meek: for they shall inherit the earth.

Blessed are they which do hunger and thirst after righteousness: for they shall be filled (Matt. 5:3-6).

When the Lord had finished the entire Sermon on the Mount to his two listeners, the Preacher butted in. Not, as you might think, with words of appreciation but a verbal scolding: "Where in the world have you been? Do you know how many people in Bigtown were disappointed? Do you realize how this stunt of yours is going to hurt church attendance, all over this county?"

Jesus looked at the Preacher, not in judgment, but in pity, "I came not to call the righteous, but sinners to repentance. . . . My kingdom is not of this world."

A few days later the Preacher tried to describe the dream to some friends at church. But a strange, quizzical look on their faces forced him to stop—and change the subject—long before he finished.

The Ten O'Clock Funeral

"Hello, Preacher? This is the Tinyburg Funeral Home. One of your members died last night—Miss Grace. They want the funeral at your church Thursday afternoon at 2:00. Can you conduct the service?"

After jotting the details on his appointment book, the Preacher thought back to a conversation he'd had with Miss Grace, about three years ago. She'd asked him to stop by her apartment, where she lived in retirement.

Miss Grace, never married, worked forty years as a bookkeeper for the Tinyburg Furniture Store. She was such a familiar figure around town that nearly everyone called her "Miss Grace." Some who called her that never knew her last name.

"I realize the sun's going down in the West for me," Miss Grace had told the Preacher that fall afternoon in her apartment, "and I want to plan my funeral. Since my only close relative is a nephew, Tom Rendleman, who lives way off in Albuquerque, I want the satisfaction of knowing my wishes will be carried out."

"Why Miss Grace, you'll probably outlive me," the Preacher answered, good-naturedly. "But if I'm still around, I'll do what you say."

"There are four things I want done," she said. "They're simple, but important to me.

61

"First, I want you to bring a brief message from the third chapter of Ecclesiastes, 'To every thing there is a season, . . . A time to weep, and a time to laugh.' You see, Preacher, I spent too much of my life weeping and keeping, and too little giving and laughing. For one thing, I saw how my own parents came down to their old age with practically nothing, depending on others to take care of them. I vowed a long time ago that would never happen to me, but I went to extremes. I was too close with my money. So you remind the folks to live a little as they go along. Tell them to wear this old world like a loose garment, rather than an old-timey corset with hooks and stays."

"And second," she went on, "I'd like my body to lie in state near the altar of our church from noon until two o'clock the day of the funeral. Since I have no close family, not many will come. But my church means so much to me. How many beautiful brides I've watched, at that altar. For years, I dreamed of being one myself.

"Third, I want you to read this essay, 'The Station,' which I clipped from *The Illinois Baptist,* years ago. It tells how the journey's the joy, not the final destination. It says that even adults should go barefoot oftener, ride more merry-go-rounds.

"And last," Miss Grace said, reaching for her checkbook, "I want you to take this money and deposit it in a savings account. After I'm gone, use it to pay someone's way to the Holy Land. I still regret I didn't go with you, a few summers ago, when you organized a tour to Israel. I thought I couldn't afford it. I was wrong. I'm too old to go now. But someone can go in my place. I don't care who. You can decide . . . "

Now that Miss Grace was gone, the Preacher reviewed

her wishes to make sure they were carried out.

Everything went as planned until Thursday morning, when the Preacher's phone rang about seven o'clock.

"The Funeral Home here," the mortician began. "There's been a change in Miss Grace's funeral. I just talked to her nephew out in Albuquerque. Said he's flying into Bigtown this morning, then rent a car to drive over here for the service. But he wants it changed to ten o'clock. Says he's got a sales meeting in Philadelphia tonight. Also wants the service here at the funeral home."

"Ten o'clock!" the Preacher almost screamed into the telephone. "That's an insult to Miss Grace. She wanted her body to lie in state at the church for a couple of hours. Besides, there won't be a handful there at ten o'clock, too late to get the word out. I feel like telling that Tom Rendleman to find someone else to conduct the service."

"I agree wholeheartedly," the mortician replied. "But when I told Tom about the lying in state, he said Miss Grace wouldn't know the difference. And remember, I'm in business to serve the public. And if Tom says he wants the service at midnight in the city park, I'd have to. Oh, another thing. Said he won't have time to go to the cemetery. Wants to stop by the insurance agency and the bank, sign what papers he needs to. You know that Tom is the beneficiary for all of Miss Grace's insurance.

"'Course, if you want to back out, I sometimes call on a retired minister over at Bigtown. The service wouldn't be too personal, since he doesn't know Miss Grace."

By now, the Preacher had calmed down, and he said, yes, he'd be there at ten o'clock. He had an idea.

He immediately dialed Aunt Sarah Biggs, a longtime friend and neighbor of Miss Grace.

But first, let me tell you a little about Aunt Sarah. Like Miss Grace, she never married. Some folks said she was married to the Bible."

On the surface, Aunt Sarah appeared stern and unbending. Once, when the congregation was debating whether to sponsor a church softball team, she objected, saying:

> **Let's work, not shirk;**
> **Let's pray, not play.**

A woman of simple tastes, she made all of her dresses from two basic patterns, changing only the fabrics and colors. She wore a hat and gloves to services the year round. In the summer, it was a white sailor hat with matching white gloves. In winter, a black felt hat and black gloves. Her hair was pulled back in a tight bun. And she alternated, summer and winter, wearing white oxford shoes, and black oxford shoes.

"When I go out in public, it doesn't take me all day to decide what to wear," she often said.

Yet her devotion to her church was warm and genuine. Some called her legalistic. In her heart, she knew better.

Aunt Sarah was probably the best Bible student in the church. "She makes those Bible names and places come alive," is how one of her Sunday School pupils explained it. "I just feel like I've been to Bethlehem or Jerusalem, when she finishes a lesson."

The Preacher often said that as long as Aunt Sarah was available, he needn't bother with a Bible concordance. "Call her, and she can give you chapter and verse on nearly any topic," he said.

Since Aunt Sarah was a woman who never hesitated to

speak her mind, her reaction was no surprise. "Moved the funeral to ten o'clock? Why, that's less than three hours from now. And to think how Miss Grace always had that Tom Rendleman to her house in the summers, when he was a boy. Took him wherever he wanted to go. Paid his way here and back. Always sent him home wearing a new outfit. Call that gratitude? I call Tom Rendleman a skunk, and I don't care who knows it."

"Aunt Sarah, I know all that," the Preacher butted in. "But let's pass the word around and get as many there as we can. If nothing else, let's do it for Miss Grace."

There was a long pause. The Preacher knew from experience not to interrupt when Aunt Sarah was thinking. Her imagination worked slowly, but thoroughly.

"Tell you what I'll do, Preacher. I've just put a ham in the oven—members of Miss Grace's circle bought it. We were planning lunch for Tom and other relatives at noon. 'Course, Tom won't have time to eat. So we'll share it with anyone who wants to come. And if I have my way the Funeral Home won't hold the people, come 10 o'clock."

The dust didn't settle in Aunt Sarah's kitchen for the next two hours. First, she called the community bulletin board at radio station TINY-FM. Then she set in motion her 100-woman prayer chain. This was an interfaith chain of women, who, in an emergency need, could be alerted in fifteen minutes of telephoning.

She also arranged for the church van to pick up any of the residents at the Tinyburg Nursing Home who wanted to go. As it turned out, the van had to make two trips.

As word spread throughout Tinyburg, many who hadn't planned to attend changed their minds. "Let's do it for Miss Grace," hummed the telephone lines, house to house, neighbor to neighbor.

Dental appointments were canceled, dresses went unhemmed, shopping trips to Bigtown were postponed, ironings were put off, TV programs went unwatched.

To the surprise of everyone except Aunt Sarah the funeral home was filled.

As Miss Grace had requested, the Preacher commented on the text from Ecclesiastes.

Then he read "The Station," which closes with these words:

> So stop pacing the aisles and counting the miles and peering ahead. Instead, swim more rivers, climb more mountains, kiss more babies, count more stars. Go barefoot oftener. Ride more merry-go-rounds, eat more ice cream, watch more sunsets. Life must be lived as we go along. The station will come soon enough. . . .

Before the benediction, he announced: "The women in Miss Grace's circle have lunch prepared at the church. All single or widowed persons, plus those of you from the nursing home, are invited. The church is only two blocks down the street. If you can't walk, our church van will make as many trips as necessary."

In spite of the somber occasion, the lunch was a festive occasion, as Miss Grace would have wished. The folks from the nursing home were the most appreciative.

After dessert, the Preacher said he had an announcement. Then he told about the expense-paid trip to the Holy Land and Miss Grace's savings account in the bank.

"Miss Grace left it up to me to decide who should go, and I'm pleased to announce that it's Aunt Sarah."

Aunt Sarah, caught completely off guard, blushed

deeply as all eyes turned in her direction. "No, not me!" she quickly replied. "Why, I've never even been on an airplane. Besides, I don't have the clothes. You can't just pick up and go to those Bible lands wearing what you'd wear here in Tinyburg. No, send someone else, someone younger."

Her last words were hardly out of her mouth when Uncle Billy Cutrell spoke up, "Why, Aunt Sarah, if I had a chance like that and had to, I'd go barefooted. This is too good to pass up."

But Aunt Sarah was adamant. To her, the subject was closed.

However, the same imagination that pulled off one of the biggest funerals in Tinyburg history also went to work on the late Miss Grace's bequest. So Saturday morning, she called the Preacher.

"Changed my mind," she laughed into the receiver. "Been thinking about what Uncle Billy said about going barefoot. So I've decided that if the Holy Land offer still stands, I"ll go, even if I'm the first American tourist to walk barefoot through the streets of Bethlehem and Nazareth!"

Aunt Sarah had been gone about two weeks when the Preacher received a picture postcard from Jerusalem, showing the Garden Tomb, the traditional burial place of Jesus.

In her familiar longhand, Aunt Sarah had written: "Went to the tomb this morning, and it was empty! Kindled my faith that all our tombs, someday, will be empty, too. And so long as we have that faith, I guess it matters little whether these bodies of ours ever lie in state . . . or whether our funerals are at two o'clock, or 10 o'clock, or whenever!"

But the story doesn't end there.

When an attorney opened Miss Grace's safety deposit box at the bank, he found a sketch of how she wanted her grave marker lettered. Her wishes were carried out, and if you are ever in Tinyburg, be sure to drive out to the community cemetery north of town. Turn in at the main gate and at the second intersection, turn to your right, and Miss Grace is buried in the third plot on your right. If the grass has not grown over her marker, here is what you'll read:

MISS GRACE
1893—1971

"Go Barefoot Oftener"

Strange, isn't it, that she omitted her last name? Maybe it's because she realized everyone knew her by that. Or maybe she wanted passers-by to pay more attention to the message than her name.

If you go on any June 21, you will see a lovely arrangement of red roses, brought there by Aunt Sarah from her own garden. That's the date Aunt Sarah visited the Open Tomb in Jerusalem.

Madonna and Child

Aunt Sarah Biggs could hardly wait until Sunday dinner was over to call Opal Baggett. "Do you know what's hanging in our new library-lounge?" she asked. "It's a nice print of a famous painting, called *Madonna and Child*, or something like that. Miss Grace left it to the church in her will. I'm sure you remember seeing it in her apartment—a gorgeous painting by some Italian named Filippo Lippi, in an antique gold frame. But Opal, that's no fit picture for a church. The baby Jesus isn't wearing anything—not even a little piece of cloth across you-know-where."

"Now, Opal, just think of all the innocent little girls and boys in our church. I can see them now, stopping by the library on Sundays, peeking in, punching each other, giggling.

"'Course I don't mean no disrespect for Miss Grace. A fine woman—gave me a trip to the Holy Land out of her life savings. But your husband's a picture framer, and he knows what's appropriate and what isn't."

"Yes, Aunt Sarah, what can I do about it?" interrupted Opal.

"I've asked the Preacher to let me bring it up as an item of business following the midweek service. I'm calling some of the more respectable members like you, to make sure they come.

"Notice I said 'more respectable.' You know, and I know, that all our people are respectable, at least the best they know how to be. But for those who don't know no better, it's our duty to hold the line."

Expecting the midweek service to last longer than usual, the Preacher's wife, Carol, left their younger sons, Andy and David, then ages four and seven, at home. Since the pastorium was next door, she felt secure in putting the boys to bed early, and leaving them alone. It was summertime and, with the windows open, she could keep an eye on what went on.

Although the crowd was larger than usual there were no small children, the parents fearing the topic might be too delicate. Oh, there was nine-year-old Janet, who sometimes baby-sat for Andy and David. Janet, innocent of what was coming, sat on the front row near an outside door.

After a short Bible study, the Preacher asked Aunt Sarah to say what was on her heart. After summarizing what she'd told Opal on the telephone, Aunt Sarah concluded, "And if we allow impressionable children to see such pictures in broad-open daylight, right here in our church, then I say . . . "

Just then the eyes of everyone were riveted on the side door, near where Janet was sitting. The Preacher's boys, in their pajamas, had just walked in blinking at the bright lights. And as four-year-old Andy reached up to rub his eyes, he turned loose of his pajama bottoms which fell to the floor.

Although only seconds passed, it seemed like long minutes before anyone moved. They sat there frozen in history, as if posing for an old-timey photographer. However, the silence lasted long enough for Andy to start crying.

Only Janet seemed alive enough to move. Running to Andy, she hugged him, pulled up his pajamas, and whispered in his ear, "Don't cry, Andrew. Everybody knows what a little boy's peeper looks like."

Folks there that night say Aunt Sarah's face turned every color of the rainbow. But if there was life in her face, there was no life in her tongue (which someone once said was long enough to lick a skillet in the kitchen, while she stringed beans on her front porch).

Now if you're one of those rare persons who doesn't know how a little boy looks with no clothes on, stop by the church library the next time you're in Tinyburg.

And don't be too severe with Aunt Sarah. Her methods may be tarnished, but her motives are golden.

A Bell for Bettie

For as long as anyone could remember, Carl Bradley had rung the bell at Tinyburg Church. A wood-carver by trade, his products sold widely in gift shops in a three-state area. But when someone suggested he open a gift shop right there in Tinyburg, where he could retail his products, he said no.

"I guess I'm a loner," Carl said. "I enjoy working with my hands and letting someone else deal with the public."

Although a speech defect from birth had left him without the ability to speak clearly, his hearing was excellent, and he also learned sign language. But when upset or touched by any emotion, he preferred to write notes, using a quaint spelling that reflected the way words sounded to him. For the most part Carl lived in his own little world, bounded by his workshop on weekdays and Tinyburg Church on Sundays.

Years ago, a pastor had led a commitment service emphasizing every-member participation. Carl, impressed, filled out one of the little cards.

And he did, year after year, until a simple announcement at a midweek service shattered his little world.

"I have wonderful news," the Preacher began, toward the end of the service. "One of our families has made a bequest of electronic chimes. Now we can enjoy the most

COMMITMENT CARD

I CAN *Ring the bell*

_____

_____

SIGNED *Carl Bradley*

beautiful chimes and hymns from our belfry, and all automatic. Best of all, Carl won't have to get up so early every Sunday and come down to the church in all kinds of weather."

The announcement electrified and delighted the congregation. The chimes and hymns would peal forth on weekdays, too, benefiting the entire community.

(Too, although no one mentioned it publicly, this would be a gracious way for Carl to give up his bell ringing. Arthritis in his hands had forced him to close his shop the preceding year, but everyone knew he was too proud to turn his back on the little commitment card signed so many years ago.)

Hardly anyone missed Carl after the service, for he always sat on a back row near the belfry and often left without greeting anyone. But when Sunday came and Carl didn't show up to ring the bell, the preacher knew something was wrong. Carl never missed, arthritis or no arthritis.

So early Monday morning the preacher stopped at Carl's. "Missed you yesterday," he began. "Not feeling well?"

"I wasn't home Sunday," Carl began slowly, his twisted fingers taking the place of his silent lips. "Bought me a bus ticket to Bigtown last Friday. Checked in a motel room . . . got drunk . . . came home Sunday afternoon."

Knowing Carl was joking, the preacher laughed so hard he choked, then added, "Carl, you wouldn't know how to order a drink if you wanted to. Now quit kidding. Tell me the truth."

But as he met Carl's eyes and saw mirrored there a hauntingly empty look, he knew the truth before Carl answered. Sunday *had* found him drunk in Bigtown, not in church.

"But why, Carl, after all these years?" the Preacher asked. "This is not like you. This is weird!"

Carl, reaching for a notepad, scribbled silently, "You don't nede Carl enymore."

And so the mystery dissolved. The memorial chimes had been bad news for Carl, not good. He felt unneeded, unwanted, for the only job in his church he knew how to do.

But for all his pleading, the Preacher couldn't persuade Carl to come back. "Why, you can ring the bell on Sundays as long as you're able," he reasoned. "We can play the chimes and hymns during the week. No one dreamed you'd be hurt."

Carl's only response was to underline what he'd written: "You don't nede Carl enymore."

And so the months passed, but Carl's pew continued vacant, and the bell rope hung limp on the hook near the front entrance. True, the chimes pealed forth, but to many, knowing Carl's feelings, they sounded more like a funeral dirge than melodies of joy.

Ten days before Christmas, the Preacher and Uncle Billy "Told-you-so" Cutrell were having coffee in the church office when a long-distance call came through from a therapist in Bigtown.

"Hello, Reverend, you don't know me, but I've got a patient who grew up in Tinyburg. Has amnesia in the worst way. Doesn't even know her name. She's Bettie Wollaver. Ever hear of her?"

"Ever since she was a little girl," the Preacher replied. "But I haven't seen her in years, since she finished high school."

"I know it's a long shot," the therapist continued, "but we want to bring Bettie back to Tinyburg and expose her to some of her earliest and happiest experiences. If we can establish a base in her memory in which she recalls just one facet, we might build on that and eventually lead her to recovery."

"What I remember best about Bettie is how she'd come early to watch Carl Bradley, our bell ringer," the Preacher continued. "Sometimes Carl would hold her in one arm and let her tug the rope. Tickled her to death. She did that 'til she was a big girl, way up in grade school."

When the therapist said he'd like to be in Tinyburg on Sunday with Bettie and let her watch Carl, the Preacher explained that Carl hadn't been to church in months. "But I'll try to talk him into it," he said as he hung up.

"Now, Preacher, before you go down to Carl's and get him all worked up, let me remind you that I told the church folks not to install that automatic music-playing machine," Uncle Billy said. "And now you're gonna make things worse. When you start tinkerin' around with a person's thinkin' cap, no telling where it'll lead—maybe a lawsuit against the church, who knows? If you want my advice, tell that therapist to keep his theraping in Bigtown."

Thanking Billy for his advice, which was about as free as Christmas trees on December 26, the preacher hurried to Carl's. But Carl was just as skeptical as Uncle Billy. "Sounds like you folks are trying to trick me into something, right here at Christmas," he replied. "Besides, anyone knows it's one chance in a million that ringing a bell could cure anyone's amnesia."

"OK, let's assume it's a lost cause. But tell me one thing—would you do it one more time, just for Bettie?" Carl, silent and pensive, then halfheartedly, replied, "I'll let you know by morning."

Early the next morning a neighbor boy knocked at the Preacher's house with a note which read:

Sunday morning, the therapist stood beside Bettie in

the foyer as Carl, his hands swollen from arthritis, reached for the rope. If there was a glint of recognition in her eyes, no one could tell. After each tug at the rope, while Carl waited for the recoil, the therapist would whisper in Bettie's ear, "The bell-ringer!" And thus, back and forth, the tolling of the bell, the whispering in her ears.

And then, miracle of miracles, Bettie rushed to Carl's side, throwing her arms around him, and together they pulled and pulled and pulled, and the bell rang and rang and rang, until everyone all over Tinyburg wondered if there might be a fire or other emergency. But it was only the fire of Christmas.

Finally, exhausted, both turned loose of the rope just as the organist began the prelude:

> I heard the bells on Christmas day
> Their old familiar carols play,
> And wild and sweet the words repeat
> Of peace on earth, good-will to men.

> HENRY WADSWORTH LONGFELLOW

And even Uncle Billy had to hurriedly wipe a tear, when he thought no one was looking.

. . . Carl lived for several years after this, resuming his old job once he was convinced the people really cared. And since his death the church continues to use volunteers on Sundays to ring the bell, playing the electronic chimes only on weekdays.

If you're ever in Tinyburg on a Sunday, get there early enough to hear the bell. And if you're there on a weekday, stop by Uncle Billy's, who lives just across the street. He has a key to the church, and he'll be glad to show you where the rope hangs in the foyer. Nearby is a simple plaque, and I hope you'll take time to read it:

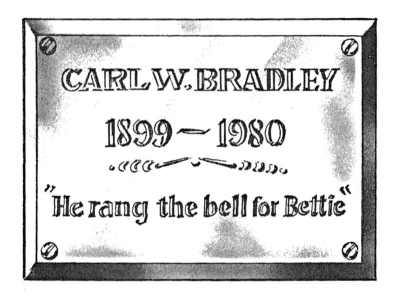

CARL W. BRADLEY

1899 — 1980

"He rang the bell for Bettie"

The TV Antenna

Whenever I visit Tinyburg, I make it a point to eat breakfast at the Tinyburg Cafe. And if possible, I sit at the table with Fred "Fixit" Turner, who's a walking encyclopedia about this little community.

One morning Fred told me about the preacher they had back in the early fifties, when television first became common.

I've forgotten his name, but anyway, the pastor at that time probably had less formal education than any preacher who'd ever served there. But what he lacked in schooling, he made up in persistence. "We've got a preacher who can do anything," was a common remark around town.

He learned mainly by imitating persons more skilled than he. For example, when he started a church newsletter, he wrote fifty of the stronger congregations in the state, asking for a sample of their bulletins.

Spreading these out before him, he took the best ideas and designed a mail out that won first place in a competition sponsored by a church advertising agency.

"It's never embarrassed me to admit that my best help comes from persons a lot smarter than I am," he often admitted.

So when he needed a new television antenna, he

installed his own, although he'd never even held one in his hand.

Since his neighbor was a television repairman, he decided to put up one just like his, and in the same manner.

His neighbor was generous with his advice, but knowing the Preacher's pride in his self-sufficiency he didn't offer to help, although he'd have been glad to.

The Preacher first drilled the lead-in hole in the same spot, secured the base, and turned the antenna facing the exact direction of his neighbor's. Then he stood off at a distance to survey his work and make a final comparison. Only then did he notice that one arm of his neighbor's antenna made a 45° turn, pointing downward.

Not to be outdone, the pastor got his ladder out of the garage and climbed back on the roof. Then, eyeing his neighbor's antenna so he would do it just right, he bent the corresponding arm at the same angle.

"Preacher, you did a good job," his neighbor observed, "but why did you buy an antenna with one bent arm?" To his chagrin, the pastor learned that the repairman's boys had damaged his antenna while playing 'andy-over with a basketball. He'd never bothered to straighten it, even though it weakened his TV signal.

That night, the Preacher had a strange dream. He was standing at his pulpit preaching away, but no one was listening. Not a soul. A couple of boys on the front row were sailing paper airplanes. A choir member was writing thank-you notes for a recent baby shower. Two families were reading the Sunday papers, their youngsters fighting over the comics. Uncle Billy Told-You-So was nodding, and another deacon was listening to a transistor radio. The ushers had set up a table in the foyer and were playing checkers.

No one—absolutely no one—was listening, not even his wife, busy with her macramé.

With a sigh of futility, he closed his Bible and left the pulpit. On the way out, he picked a bud from a vase of flowers on the communion table. Before reaching for his hat, he stooped over for a drink at the water fountain. As usual, the cooler spurted unexpectedly, dousing his eyes with water, which he wiped with his handkerchief.

But the drama wasn't over. Looking back, he was amazed to see that the congregation was leaving too, single file, much like a funeral or wedding. Each stopped to select a flower, each stopped for a drink, and each wiped his eyes with a handkerchief.

"Whatever caused such a crazy dream?" he asked his wife at the breakfast table, not really expecting an answer.

It was two or three mornings later before he pieced together his experience with the broken antenna and his dream of the sleeping congregation. It happened while he was reading 1 Corinthians 9:27, "I am my body's sternest master, for fear that when I have preached to others I should myself be disqualified" (Phillips).

He recalled also a definition he once read in the book, *A Spiritual Autobiography* by William Barclay, to the effect that preaching is "truth through personality."

On an impulse, he cut out the Bible verse and taped it to the flyleaf of his Bible. On the same page he taped a J. C. Penney newspaper ad for television antennas.

And as long as he was pastor there, he inevitably glanced at that flyleaf just before he entered the pulpit as a reminder that his example far outweighed his sermons.

The Tinyburg Church has a beautiful tradition, handed down through the years. When a pastor leaves, he gives his pulpit Bible to their library, and the congregation in turn presents him with a new one.

These old Bibles rest on the "preachers' shelf" in the library, and members, especially the older ones, frequently stop by to leaf through one. They don't check them out to read, but just to hold and reminisce.

Now, if you're ever in Tinyburg on a Sunday, be sure to stop by the church library. It's on the first floor of their new educational unit, near the north entrance. Browse for a few minutes at the preachers' shelf, and be sure to ask for this one and open to the flyleaf. The J. C. Penney ad is yellowed with time, but it's still there, along with the Corinthian verse.

It should be easy to find, for I'm told members ask for it more than any, and the covers are beginning to fray.

. . .

A Thanksgiving to Remember

"Preacher, this is the coroner talking. Say, we've got a fellow over here at the Tinyburg Funeral Home to bury. There won't be a service—just someone to say a prayer at the cemetery. Are you free?" It was the Monday before Thanksgiving.

On the ride out in the hearse, the funeral director picked up the story. "This fellow's a suicide," he told the Preacher. "Found him in a room which he'd rented upstairs over Smith's Pharmacy. When we called his family out East, they refused to come or have anything to do with him. Didn't even send a flower.

"Seems he was a drifter. Not a bad fellow, but just couldn't settle down. Strange, though, there was a big pile of letters stuffed in his footlocker, to and from his family.

"The funny thing is he'd written all those letters himself. He wrote to himself as if he were his parents. Then he'd answer their letters. But none ever got mailed. You could tell the handwriting was all the same.

"The last few letters talked about Thanksgiving and how he looked forward to coming home and how they wanted him to come. But it was all in his head."

The Preacher thought for a few minutes. "Evidently," he sighed, "here was a fellow who wanted a family and to be with them. Since, for some reason, that was impossible, he made up his own dream world. In his mind, he was really going home for Thanksgiving."

Three mourners stood at the open grave—the mortician, the coroner, the minister. The freshly turned dirt, muddy from a recent shower, stuck to their shoes. The cheap, wooden coffin, covered with a grey, clothlike material, matched the grey of the November skies.

The coroner asked the mortician to open the casket one more time, for final identification. There was nothing in the forty-year-old face that said who he was, or why he was, or whence he was.

The Preacher quoted:

"What is man, that thou art mindful of him? and the son of man, that thou visitest him?" (Ps. 8:4).

"When my father and my mother forsake me, then the Lord will take me up" (Ps. 27:10).

That night, three men in Tinyburg made long distance calls. The Preacher dialed a distant uncle who had paid his first semester's tuition in college.

The mortician called his father in a faraway nursing home, even though the elderly man was too confused to know who it was that called.

The coroner talked to his son in college, who would be having Thanksgiving dinner with his fiancee in another state.

Each called to say three words, "I love you." But each choked up before he reached even the second word.

At the community Thanksgiving service on Thursday morning, the Preacher described the drifter's death. He explained how this fellow dreamed of closeness and intimacy with his family and how he created a make-believe world in a vain effort to make his dream come true.

"He wanted not so much what his family could give him, but his family itself," the Preacher concluded. "And today, as we praise our Heavenly Father, let's include a petition for closeness with him, more so than for material gifts.

And here was his closing prayer at the community service:

> Gracious Father, as the mantle of winter casts its shadow across the fading flowers and fruits of fall, we pause to praise thee for the long days of summer when under cloudless skies the fields brought forth their bounty.
>
> Merciful Father, as we revel in the material bounties of thy hand, may we also be grateful for thy goodness that hath created us, thy love that hath redeemed us, thy providence that shelters us, thy discipline that chastens us, and thy patience that bears with us.
>
> Generous father, give us more. Give us hearts to love and praise thee, minds to know thee, wills to serve thee, feet to follow thee, eyes to see thee, hands to serve thee.
>
> But most of all, give us of thyself. Without thee, the "fields strive in vain to look gay." The whole world is a mere trinket, a trifle. It is thee—and not thy gifts—for which we crave. Amen.

Should you visit Tinyburg, you might, out of curiosity, want to stop by the drifter's grave. But there's no use trying. I've looked for it myself, but it went unmarked and is now unknown.

What hasn't gone unmarked, however, is the Preacher's prayer, "It is thee—and not thy gifts—for which we crave." That Thanksgiving morning, many listeners asked for copies, some of which found their way into family Bibles, pressed there for future reflection, along with other mementos that make one day stand out above others.

His Mother's Prayer

Greg Thompson was not the first young man from Tinyburg Church to enter the ministry. But he was the first to study overseas, to earn a doctorate at Oxford University.

So the first Sunday he was back in Tinyburg following graduation, plans were made for him to deliver the morning sermon.

Greg's father died when he was thirteen, and his mother had passed away during his final year of study at Oxford. So the weekend in Tinyburg, he was a guest in the home of his mother's sister, Opal Baggett, and her husband Earl.

He felt much at home with the Baggetts, for Earl had been more like a father than an uncle, and Opal was his second mother.

Opal and Earl lived in an old but comfortable house, that once boasted a fireplace in every room. Opal fixed his bed in the guest room, and Earl carried in a study table and lamp for Greg's last-minute sermon preparation.

Saturday morning about eleven o'clock, Opal peeked in Greg's room, bringing a cup of hot apple cider and his favorite oatmeal cookies made with raisins. She was

almost awed with the big reference books which Greg
had spread out on his study table.

"Oh, Greg, we're so proud of you," she said. "You've
always been the scholar in the family. Best of all, it never
went to your head. Since you learned to read, books were
a favorite with you. But they never kept you from being a
real boy and making friends on your basketball team and
in your youth group at church."

"It's true I've always liked books," Greg replied, biting
off a chewy piece of cookie. "But I'm not sure about that
scholar business. Folks around here probably think I
know a lot more than I do. That's why I'm doing all this
research on my sermon for tomorrow. I plan to quote
several authorities on theology and church history. Also,
I want to include some word study, based on the Greek
and Hebrew manuscripts."

Opal hesitated before continuing, lest she be misun-
derstood. Then, gathering courage, she asked, "Greg, do
you remember what your mother said when you were
growing up? I heard her say it so many times: 'Greg, if
the Lord ever calls you to preach, be sure to say a good
word for Jesus Christ.'"

Greg nodded while two big tears blinded him tem-
porarily. "How could I ever forget?" he answered.

About 3:00 that afternoon, Greg stepped out to the
little shop in the back, where Uncle Earl did his picture
framing. Years ago, Earl began framing photographs
and paintings as a hobby. He got so good at it that now,
during retirement, customers kept him busy at least two
days a week. "I guess I could do picture framing seven
days a week, if I took all the business I'm offered," he
often said.

Greg was fascinated with a print of Sallman's *Head of*

Christ, which his uncle was working on. "Look here how the color of the wood frame highlights the golden sheen on the Lord's hair," Earl pointed out. "I'm devoting special pains to this one, for it's a gift for our church, maybe to hang in the library."

"Uncle Earl, let's go for a walk out to Thompson's Woods," Greg said, wanting a break from his sermon preparation. So Earl put away the painting, and off the two went to the scene of Greg's favorite hideout as a boy.

"I wonder why so many folks come to you for their framing," Greg asked as they walked through the woods, quiet with winter. "Did you take special training or stumble on to some secret?"

"I guess I've always had a knack for working with wood," his uncle responded. "But my secret—if you want to call it that—is something I learned from a real craftsman. He told me, 'Earl, never let the frame overshadow the picture. Select your woods, your stains, your matting, so they will highlight your print or paint-ing. It's like a vase of beautiful flowers—you never allow a vase to steal the show.'"

"He went on to warn me that if a customer bragged, 'Earl, what a gorgeous frame,' instead of, 'Oh, what a beautiful painting,' that I'd failed."

"I'd never thought of it that way," Greg replied, "but it sure makes sense."

It was early January, the days were short, and dusk came quickly. Before they got back to the house, the first stars appeared. Over in the west, they spotted a falling star which brought to mind an old saying Uncle Earl used to hear when he was a boy: "A falling star is a tear from the eyes of God, shed for the sins of the world."

While they were gone, Aunt Opal had kindled a fire in

the grate in Greg's room. Its flickering flames cast a warm, emotional glow over Greg's memory; for before the Baggetts put in central heating, they always built a fire in this room when he stayed overnight.

After supper, trying to review his sermon notes, the words of his aunt and uncle kept reverberating in his mind:

If the Lord calls you to preach, be sure to say a good word for Jesus Christ.

Never let the frame overshadow the picture.

Then, drawing a deep sigh, he picked up his sermon manuscript—filled with quotes from this doctor and that professor—walked over to the grate and dropped it into the fire. The flames greedily devoured such choice phrases as "the Deutero-Isaiah problem" and the "ancient Semitic influences." As he watched his papers glow with reds and bright orange, then curl up into powdery ashes, he wondered if he'd have anything to say, come Sunday morning. . . .

Nearly every pew was filled, for it was a proud day for all of Tinyburg. A larger than usual number of visitors came to hear Greg, including some of his high school teachers, as well as two distant relatives and their families from out of town. Those who had watched Greg grow up in the church, including some who had cared for him as a baby in the nursery, waited with special anticipation. Every listener was in Greg's corner.

Speaking without notes, Greg spoke simply on "The Light of the World," describing the Son of God as the answer to man's darkest moments, "the tear of God that falls in the night for our sins." In doing so he drew on his study of the original languages, an occasional quote from a learned theologian, with bits of church history and

biblical archaeology thrown in for good measure.

But in every sentence the Lord himself shown through, framed and accented by the fruits of Greg's years of study.

For a closing illustration he chose not a scholarly gem of some church father, but this testimony from sawdust-trail evangelist Billy Sunday:

> I entered through the portico of Genesis and walked down through the long, Old Testament art gallery, where I saw hanging on the walls, hundreds of paintings of such persons as Adam and Eve, Cain and Abel, Melchizedek and Methuselah, Abraham and Isaac, Jacob and Esau, Joseph and Benjamin, Moses and Aaron, Sampson and Delilah, Esther and Ruth, Daniel and Nebuchadnezzar. I stepped then into the music room of the Psalms, where every reed of God's great organ responded to the tuneful harp of David.
>
> I walked then into the business office of the Proverbs, and the chamber of Ecclesiastes where the voice of the Preacher was heard, and into the conservatory of Sharon, where the lily of the valley's spices filled and perfumed my life.
>
> Then I entered into the observation rooms of the prophets, where I saw telescopes of various sizes, some pointing to far-off events, but all centered upon the bright star which was to rise above the moonlit hills of Judea for our salvation.
>
> Leaving the Old Testament, I then stepped into the correspondence rooms where sat Matthew, Mark, Luke, John, Peter, Paul, and James penning their epistles.
>
> I stopped then in the Jerusalem Travel Agency, where I saw mission travel brochures, some with sailing dates and others with caravan schedules, but all with such First Century destinations as Judea and Samaria, Corinth and Ephesus, Antioch and Cypress,

> Philippi and Thessalonica, Berea and Crete, Galatia
> and Malta, Athens and Rome.
> Finally, I stepped into the throne room of Revelation
> where I caught a vision of the King sitting on his
> throne in all his glory, and I cried, "Let angels pros-
> trate fall, bring forth the royal diadem, and crown him
> Lord of all."

His sermon ended, the congregation sat motionless a
few seconds, unwilling to break the spell of what they
had heard.

At the door, Uncle Billy Cutrell said, "Greg, don't let
this go to your head, but that was one of the clearest
sermons I ever heard, and I've listened to a lot in my day.
Somethin' different about yours . . . didn't feel as if I was
listenin' to a sermon so much as lookin' at a pretty
picture. In fact, I told you seven years ago you were a
good preacher and didn't need to waste all these years
going away to school."

At the dinner table Aunt Opal said, "Greg, your mother
would have been pleased; you answered her prayer."

"All I did," Greg replied, "was to remember what
Uncle Earl said—that a picture is more important than
its frame."

Ten days later the church got a letter from Greg,
thanking them for hearing him preach. Then he added, "I
understand my Uncle Earl is giving Sallman's *Head of
Christ* to the church, a print which he framed himself.
May I suggest that instead of hanging it in the library,
you display it on the back wall of the sanctuary, in line
with the Preacher's eyes. There it can be a constant
reminder to every minister that 'saying a good word for
Jesus Christ' is what it's all about."

And so they did.

When you visit Tinyburg, stop by the church and see the painting. If you can't be there on a Sunday, remember that Uncle Billy Cutrell, who lives across the street, has a key. He'd be tickled to death to let you in and might even reminisce about Greg's sermon, for folks still talk about it.

Be sure to walk up onto the rostrum, turn around, and study the painting from that perspective. Then let your eyes drop to the pulpit, which is on a direct line with the head of Christ. Here engraved, are these words from John 3:30:

He must increase, but I must decrease.

I've never heard them myself, but I understand at this point Uncle Billy usually turns on the electronic chimes, programmed to play the music to the closing words of Greg's sermon:

All hail the pow'r of Jesus' name!
Let angels prostrate fall;
Bring forth the royal diadem,
And crown him Lord of all.

EDWARD PERRONET

One More Christmas Card

The letter, written with a trembling hand, came addressed to the postmaster. "Dear Sir or Madam," it began. "I grew up in Tinyburg where I taught the third grade for many years. Now I am an old woman. My mind has outlived my body, and I've survived most of my friends.

"Here in Ohio, I live in a beautiful retirement home. I have no material needs, and during the holidays we will enjoy many lovely parties and entertainments. But I was thinking what I would most like for Christmas. It would be one more Christmas card with a Tinyburg postmark!

"To me, there can never be another Tinyburg. I loved the children I taught, and they loved me. No one there was perfect, but we accepted each other for what we were. I loved my church, my neighbors, the quiet streets. I loved the hush of Christmas, which always fell like a quiet benediction on our village. And oh, how I would like to hear Carl Bradley ring the church bell like he used to, on Christmas Sunday. I was there, years ago, when he rang the bell the Christmas Sunday that Bettie Wollaver recovered from her amnesia.

"So I'm enclosing one dollar. If it's not too much trouble, would you buy a card—a simple one is OK—and mail it from the post office there? I may seem like a silly old woman to you. But to me, the Tinyburg postmark will kindle the memories of over seventy Christmases I enjoyed there. Signed, Helen Norman."

The Tinyburg postmaster, who prides himself on his self-composure, was surprised and somewhat embarrassed by a sudden tear that fell on the lilac-scented stationery.

And since he was not given to impulsiveness, he further surprised himself by dialing the Preacher. "Reverend," he began, "why don't we send that teacher over in Ohio a mountain of cards from Tinyburg? And if anyone can pull it off, you can."

Nothing pleased the Preacher more than a request to do the unusual (finding a billy goat to pull a child's wagon at the school carnival). Or, the impossible (raising money to pay the medical bills of the town drunk who broke both legs trying to play Superman).

So within minutes, it was done. He prepared notices for all the church bulletins in town, arranged for an announcement over the school's PA system, wrote a story for the *Tinyburg Times*, and called in to the community bulletin board of radio station TINY-FM.

When the first cards arrived, Helen was elated. Actually, the envelopes with the Tinyburg postmark pleased her more than the cards. But as the trickle grew into a deluge, she was at a loss what to do with all of them. She had already stood every possible card on her dresser and bedside table, and taped the envelopes all over her door, and even her mirror.

Then she had an idea. She, too, would play postmistress! So she readdressed the cards to her fellow patients, while the nurses' aides delivered them to every room. And by Christmas morning, Tinyburg adorned every door, every mirror, every table in the retirement home.

For once, Tinyburg had eclipsed Bethlehem!

A Valentine from Tiger

The kids called him Tiger. Where he came from, no one ever bothered to ask. But there he was, wagging his tail, right in front of the Tinyburg Church every Sunday morning, and licking the hands of all who would let him.

(Aunt Sarah Biggs, who lived in constant dread of "coming down with something," warned of the dire results. "By the time that dog licks everyone's hands, then we all shake hands with each other, just imagine the germs floating around this church," she moaned. Her solution was to wear gloves, the year around.)

Most folks assumed that Tiger knew when it was Sunday by the ringing of the church bell. But Uncle Billy Cutrell, who lives across the street and is up early every Sunday, said lots of times Tiger showed up, long before the first bell. And just as no one knew where Tiger came from, so no one knew where he spent the rest of the week.

The members tolerated Tiger, if for no other reason than that he was so friendly. His world knew no strangers. With his white feet, and white and yellow stripes on his body, he was as familiar a figure as Carl Bradley, the bell ringer. And just as faithful, regardless of the weather. He never took a vacation!

Tiger—or no one else—had any way of knowing how

101

much disagreement would come from one little article in the *Tinyburg News*. "Tinyburg Selected for Halfway House," read the headline. The story told how the state department of corrections was renting a big home in Tinyburg, where eight prisoners would be housed in a work-release program.

The article went on to explain that one reason for choosing Tinyburg was its small-town atmosphere and friendliness. It was seen as a community where men nearing the end of their prison terms could find jobs and acceptance, before going out on their own.

Some citizens thought otherwise, but there was no organized resistance—just talk about the danger of known criminals actually living next door to normal people.

Shortly after the house opened, the resident counselor stopped by Tinyburg Church to ask the Preacher if it would be OK for the men to visit the next Sunday.

"We can't make them attend regularly, but they did promise to come one Sunday," the counselor explained. "Now we won't march them in, or anything like that. They'll be dressed like anybody else and come in groups of two or three, maybe one by himself. And naturally, we don't want any reserved seats. If these men adapt to society, the community must take them at face value and not make a fuss, either way."

When the Preacher said the members would welcome the men, he didn't reckon with Rick "Six-Percent" Hardy.

To understand why Rick Hardy opposed the eight men visiting Tinyburg Church, you've got to know more about him. Rick had been a loan officer at the Tinyburg National Bank for over twenty years. Extremely efficient and hardworking, his chief ambition was to be named vice-president with an office of his own.

He had an uncanny ability to size up applicants for loans, seldom misjudging their ability to repay. Also, he had memorized several tables of payment schedules. Without an adding machine, he could usually quote the monthly payments on any given loan, at various interest rates. Long after electronic calculators became common, he was the last bank employee to use one. That's how he got the nickname "Six Percent" although hardly anyone ever called him that to his face, for it infuriated him no end. Oh, a couple of town loafers weren't intimidated, for whenever they saw him coming down Main Street they'd raise their voices, "Here comes old Six Percent!"

But the bank directors hesitated to promote him because of his negativism. He knew his repayment schedules, but he didn't know people. He seldom smiled at anyone. He was efficient, but in a cold sort of way.

His best friend at church was Aunt Sarah Biggs, who often quoted her favorite motto:

> **Let's work,**
> **not shirk;**
> **Let's pray,**
> **not play.**

And she was fond of saying, "Brother Hardy, every church needs someone to take a stand, to hold the line, to say 'this is enough.' And I feel deep in my soul that you're the man of the hour." This only made him determined that once he'd made up his mind, never to change, especially over a moral issue.

So when Rick Hardy learned that as many as eight soon-to-be released prisoners might the very next Sunday be rubbing shoulders with innocent children, virtuous women, and stalwart men, he went immediately to the church office.

"Preacher," he began, without even sitting down, "if you're the man of God you claim to be, you'll be standing on the front steps Sunday morning with your arms folded. And when those jailbirds start up the steps, you'll tell them, 'Sorry, fellows, but the church's full!'"

"The church is full? What do you mean, Rick, we've always got room."

"I mean we don't have room for the likes of them, that's what I mean," Rick replied. "You don't have to say what the church is full of, just that it's full. That's a polite way of saying we don't have room for misfits. Our pews were never intended for ex-cons, coming in here all dressed up in white shirts, looking so religiouslike. Truth is, they ought to wear denim shirts, stenciled *Convict 026932* or whatever on the back."

"Rick, I stand in this pulpit every Sunday and try to preach the Word of God, which welcomes all men," the Preacher continued.

"Oh, does it?" Rick asked sarcastically. "You got a Bible there? Open it to the Book of Matthew, chapter 21, verse 13, and read it to me."

Quickly thumbing to Matthew, the Preacher read aloud, "My house shall be called the house of prayer; but ye have made it a den of thieves."

"But Rick, that wasn't what Jesus was talking about," the Preacher said. "You're twisting that verse all out of context."

"I'm not twistin' anything; I'm just standing on the Good Book, and it says God's house is not for thieves."

"Well, if you want to get personal, all of us are thieves,

one way or another. If sinners can't attend, every pew would be empty."

But Rick had an answer: "Yes, Preacher, but there's a difference in *penitentiary* sinners and respectable sinners. Why, you take our folks, they're all good people. Oh, someone might lose his temper now and then, say a cuss word or something. But we're moral people, and the Bible commands us to be separate and not mix and mingle with all the riffraff that comes along. I like to think that Tinyburg is at least six or seven miles from any known source of what you'd call real sin.

"And another thing," Rick continued. "I've seen fellows like these come in the bank, asking change for a five-dollar bill. Why, they can confuse a teller so fast that they walk out with fifty dollars in change! And mind me when the collection plate's passed, any one of those fellows can put in a one-dollar bill and pull out a twenty and no one be the wiser."

The Preacher drew a deep breath, then choked back words begging to be said. He knew that even if he won the argument with "Six Percent," he'd lose the battle.

The next Sunday morning, Tiger showed up, right on time, wagging his tail, first licking the hands of Carl Bradley the bell ringer. And one by one, as others arrived by car or on foot, Tiger met each one, eager to lick the hands of anyone who would oblige him.

All eight men in the work-release program came, too. Six came in pairs, and two walked singly. Grant Sizemore was one of the eight who entered the church alone. Not only did Grant allow Tiger to lick his hand, but he knelt beside him, stroking his ears and tickling his belly as he rolled over.

For his sermon that morning, the Preacher didn't plan

to single out the eight visitors, yet he wanted to urge his congregation to be compassionate. So he preached on the rich man and Lazarus from Luke's Gospel.

"Lazarus was not only a beggar, but he was also a sick man, his body covered with running sores," the Preacher began. "Nearby was a rich man, who could at least have fed him crumbs from his table. But he thought only about himself. The only help the beggar got was from some dogs, who 'came and licked his sores'" (Luke 16:21).

Rick Hardy squirmed in his pew until his wife, who long ago gave up offering any advice, dared to whisper that he was acting like a child. And Aunt Sarah Biggs tugged at her gloves, repeatedly taking them off and putting them on as if she didn't know whether to stay or leave.

Otherwise, the service was routine.

In the weeks ahead, Grant Sizemore was the only one of the eight who came back with any regularity. (For once, Uncle Billy Cutrell echoed the sentiments of Rick Hardy by saying, "I told you those fellows wouldn't stick.")

In fact, Grant not only came on Sundays, but also to weekday activities. He even played several games on the church softball team. And he and Tiger became almost inseparable. In fact, the second Sunday, Tiger followed him home after church. Since no one seemed to know who the dog belonged to, Grant's counselor told Grant he could keep Tiger at the halfway house.

So although Tiger had been only a Sunday "member," his church activities really picked up that summer; for wherever Grant went, Tiger tagged along.

Six months passed, and it was time for Grant Sizemore to be released. He had a job waiting in his hometown in southeast Missouri, and as much as he liked Tinyburg he could hardly wait for his discharge date.

The last Sunday in Tinyburg, Grant asked if he could say a word to the congregation.

"I'm not much of a talker," he began, fumbling nervously with a ball-point pen in his hand. "But I just want to thank you folks for what you've done. Most of all, I want to thank Tiger, for he reminds me of the dog I had when I was a boy, always licking my hand, warm and soft.

"That seems so long ago, for I got away from pets and rubber-tire swings and summer swimmin' holes for the fast life. I fell in with the wrong crowd, listened to the wrong voices. But you folks—and Tiger, well, you stirred something inside me which I thought died a long time ago. I figure I'm not too old to start over, to be a boy again, get me a dog and a fishin' pole, and a rifle to hunt rabbits.

"Too, I want to thank the Preacher for his first sermon, about the dog licking the sores of that old beggar, Lazarus. I was a beggar, and Tiger licked my hurt feelings. Oh, not literally, but he touched me. And you folks touched me. And most of all . . . the Lord touched me."

After a long pause, when even the Preacher fumbled for words, Uncle Billy Cutrell asked for the floor. "Folks," he began, "I told you six months ago we had nothing to fear from these new fellows. It's not that I'm boasting that I was right and some of you were wrong, but that I'm bragging on our town, and on our citizens, and yes, on a stray dog by the name of Tiger.

"And that leads me to what I really got up here to say. Since Tiger just appeared out of nowhere, that means he belongs to our church as much as anybody, for he never misses. So I'd like to suggest, much as we'll miss him, that we let Grant take Tiger home with him to Missouri."

And so it was.

For a few Sundays, especially, the children missed Tiger. Some wondered if the church might adopt another dog, until Uncle Billy pointed out that no one adopts dogs; they adopt you!

However, everyone felt better in February when a Valentine arrived for the church bulletin board signed, "We love you—Grant and Tiger." Enclosed was a snapshot of the two, made out in a field when they were hunting rabbits. Also enclosed was a handwritten note. It was unsigned, except that Grant had apparently rubbed ink on Tiger's paw, then made a print of it at the bottom. It consisted of only fifteen words: "We're doing great. And best of all, Grant lets me lick his hands every day!"

And even Six Percent Hardy, when he saw it, had to bite his lips to hold back an uninvited tear.

The Banker Who Played God

Rick "Six-Percent" Hardy, loan officer at the Tinyburg Bank, was the last employee to get an electronic calculator. "Since I've memorized the payment schedule for any loan, from six to sixteen percent interest, those gadgets are just a botheration," is how he put it.

Rick Hardy's big ambition was an office of his own and title of vice-president. He resented his small desk, just off the lobby. But bank directors knew he was too abrasive, too nosy, too penny conscious for a promotion.

Frustrated at work, Rick found release from stress by throwing his weight around at the Tinyburg Church. Several years back, he won the undying friendship of Aunt Sarah Biggs when he took her side, opposing a church softball league. He said a loud amen when Aunt Sarah warned that ball games would keep the young folks out of prayer meeting. He pleased her more by making reprints on the bank photocopier of her oft-repeated motto:

> Let's work, not shirk,
> Let's pray, not play;
> Let's build the church,
> Not boost the games.

"Mr. Hardy, when you take a stand like this, I feel as if

you're God himself, up there defending our faith," she told him.

Rick Hardy had never liked the Preacher. Fact is, he distrusted any minister. "Most of them don't know the value of a dollar," he observed. "Never accumulate anything, just live week to week, always talking about giving to this or that."

So it was almost with pleasure that he accosted the Preacher one December morning in his study. "Reverend, I'm going to level with you. Just learned that last summer, on your vacation, you and the Mrs. saw an X-rated movie in Bigtown."

"So what?" the Preacher asked.

"So what? So what? So what?" Rick mimicked him, with sarcasm in his voice. "I'll tell you what. It's an inexcusable sin against humanity and God Almighty. But if you promise to resign tomorrow night, you'll have thirty days to vacate the pastorium. That's what our constitution allows. If not, I'll tell the whole church and declare the pulpit vacant."

The Preacher turned white. "Rick," he pleaded, "I won't deny going. But it was an impulsive thing. After all, I'm a man like you. We were with another couple who said every minister should see at least one X-rated movie. You know that's not our life-style—we don't see half-a-dozen movies a year of any kind."

"That's my point," Rick bristled. "You're *not* a man like anyone else. You took ordination vows, holy orders that set you apart. As a leader, I feel duty bound to keep a holy man in a holy pulpit. And our people admire me. One member said I remind her of God himself."

At first, the Preacher thought Rick was joking. Now he knew better. "December's a bad time to move," he reasoned. "I can't get another church in thirty days . . . and our boys will have to change schools in the middle of the year."

"Thirty days is thirty days," Rick replied icily.

"Suppose you bring it before the church?" the Preacher asked. "Do you have the votes to put me out on a single issue like a movie? Would the members discount everything else I stand for?"

"It's not votes, son," Rick replied, his jugular vein swelling and turning purple. "It's money, spelled m-o-n-e-y. Who do you think OK'd the mortgages for the homes that half our members live in? What about their high school kids, soon be marrying, applying for loans?

"You sit here in your office and read your little devotional books about how prayer changes things. Bah! It's dollars that change things, not prayer. Money talks in Tinyburg. Always has. Always will. Folks know my bank will be here long after you're gone.

"Another thing. I warned you back when you invited those jailbirds to our church. If you had sense to open your eyes, you'd see several black marks on your record."

"But Rick, aren't you pleased that at least one of those ex-prisoners made a new life for himself?" the Preacher responded.

"New life my foot. Track him down—I'll bet he's back in jail or else his picture's on one of them wanted posters in the post office."

Folks couldn't figure out why the Preacher just up and moved, three days after Christmas, in a U-Haul truck, leaving no forwarding address. Due to the long weekend, attendance was low on Sunday, December 27, and only a handful attended the farewell reception that night, sipping leftover punch from a children's party.

"Maybe they're having family trouble . . . leaving the ministry . . . going back to school . . . even joining another denomination," the members speculated.

"Whatever it is, it's Bad, spelled with a capital B," chimed in Uncle Billy Cutrell, shaking his head and sucking in his breath with a whistling noise that made all the women nervous.

"Don't worry yourself, Uncle Billy," advised Rick. "The world's full of preachers. Any number'd be proud to get this pulpit. We don't have to be in no hurry. I met a retired minister in Bigtown who's on Social Security— he'd be tickled to drive over on Sundays and fill in. Wouldn't expect no big salary, either. Give us a breathin' spell and a chance to catch up on our budget, too."

New Year's Eve, Rick bought his wife an expensive bottle of cologne. Ordinarily, he chose a practical gift for the kitchen on their wedding anniversary. But tomorrow was their thirtieth, and he felt like splurging. Fresh from his victory over the Preacher, he felt a new sense of virility, of self-confidence, and he decided to give her the cologne tonight.

And although he would never admit it, Rick tingled with a smidgen of pleasure as he drove by the pastorium, now dark and empty, on his way home.

The house seemed quieter than usual when he walked in, although Mrs. Hardy was by nature, both at home and in public, a shy and retiring person. If asked anything, she invariably replied, "I'm sorry, but I'll have to ask Rick. . . . " Even to her friends she always seemed to hold back, as if afraid of displeasing Rick.

Not only was the house quiet, but also dark. Flipping on a switch in their bedroom, he found a note on the dresser mirror:

**Guess I should have given you thirty days notice, but
for thirty years I've tried to tell you how hard it is to
live with God. So I've finally decided to join the human
race. Happy anniversary!**

He looked down at the dresser for their wedding
picture, but it was gone. He opened her clothes closet,
but it was bare. He glanced at the bed where their
children were conceived, but it was empty.

"(Expletive deleted)," he said. "(Four expletives deleted)."

If Rick Hardy were God, he didn't act like it now. With
satanic fury he ripped the covers off the bed and, with his
pocketknife, shredded the mattress and pillows. Moving
to the windows, he yanked the shades and curtains from
their fasteners. He emptied his own drawers and closet
and threw ties and shirts and jackets and socks helter-
skelter all over the room.

He grabbed pictures off the walls, throwing them to
the floor, stomping them to bits. Running to the refrigerator, he grabbed bottles of ketchup and mustard and
mayonnaise which he hurled against the walls of their
bedroom. Finding a hatchet in the garage, he kicked over
the bedroom dresser and hacked it to splinters.

With one final burst he threw the new bottle of cologne
against a mirror, the broken glass nicking his face and
drawing blood.

Exhausted, he stumbled to the living room, fell on the
couch, screamed another curse, then broke into convul-
sive tears.

If you've lived in a small town, I can skip the next six
weeks, for you will know how the details gradually came
to light—at the corner barbershop, in the post office,

over coffee at the Tinyburg Cafe, in whispered groups after choir practice.

I'll not detail how the members finally located the Preacher's family, of the honest discussions, of the church calling him back, of the gala welcome-home reception at an all-church Valentine's Day Party on February 14. You can fill those gaps.

What I will tell—for I find it hard to believe myself—is that Mr. and Mrs. Rick Hardy also attended the party, acting like newlyweds.

"I know you're shocked to see us," explained Rick, "especially me. It's just that New Year's Day, I inventoried my life for the first time. Oh, at the bank I'd justified and rectified and summarized right to the penny, every year.

"But I never bothered to inventory old Six-Percent Hardy, to ask who I really am. Well, I can explain one thing. When I finished with Rick, he was deep in the red. Way overdrawn.

"However, I found a way to balance my account. Don't ask me how. Just believe and forgive me. . . . "

The party closed by crowning a king and queen of sweethearts. Both Rick and his wife, and the Preacher and his wife, were strong contenders. I sure wish I knew which won. But those who were there agreed you don't have to tell everything you know, so they've kept it a secret all these years, just for fun.

An Easter to Remember

His first Sunday at Tinyburg Church, the Preacher noticed this shy fellow on the back pew who left hurriedly during benediction lest anyone speak to him. It was Theo Casey, a local accountant, and that day the Preacher determined to cultivate his friendship.

He succeeded. It wasn't long until Theo sat closer to the front, attended regularly, and occasionally served on a committee. Moreover, the two became good friends. Each July Fourth, their families enjoyed a cookout. At least once a year Theo flew the Preacher to Minnesota for a fishing trip.

Theo had done well as a self-employed accountant. A part interest in a private plane based at Bigtown airport was just one example of his prosperity. Theo was also generous, buying the Preacher a new suit almost every Easter plus occasional gifts such as a new set of golf clubs.

But more than the gifts, the Preacher relished Theo's spiritual growth. "When I see a fellow like Theo maturing in the Lord, it makes all my work worthwhile," he once confided in the Rev. Henry Moss, D.D., minister of Bigtown Church.

Theo Casey took real pride when the church elected him treasurer. With his skills as an accountant, the financial reports reflected a new accuracy and efficiency. Moreover, Theo volunteered to help the counting committee which met Sunday afternoons at 3 o'clock. The morning offerings were locked in a small safe in the office, then counted and verified in the presence of at least three persons.

Theo hadn't missed a Sunday afternoon in three years, until one January Sunday when company came in unexpectedly about 2:45. The same afternoon, before the counting committee had finished, a member rushed in the church office, almost breathless.

"Have you fellows counted the money yet? I'm missing two half dollars, rare pieces, worth about seventy-five dollars each," he explained, between breaths. "Each fifty-cent piece is a half-bust, dated 1807. Had them out last night, showing them to a friend. Laid them on the dresser, and this morning my wife picked them up and put them in the offering plate not knowing their value."

A careful search failed to locate the rare coins. "Sure your wife put them in the offering?" the counting chairman asked. "I'm dead sure, and if they're not in this offering then some monkey business is going on around here."

"Careful now, you're among friends, not thieves," the chairman replied. "If your money's here, we'll find it. If not, we'll investigate."

The committee decided to call the Tinyburg police station to ask for advice. "Whoever got those coins— assuming someone did—is likely a local person," the chief replied. "As rare as they are, they can be easily spotted. What we can do is put out a flyer to area banks and the Bigtown Coin Shop."

Still not satisfied, the coins' owner combed every

square inch of the church, looking under every pew, in every corner, every wastebasket, even under the kitchen refrigerator. But the search was fruitless. Disgusted, he returned home $150 poorer.

The weeks passed and the incident was almost forgotten when the Preacher got a phone call from the police. "Remember those 1807 half dollars? A fellow just tried to sell them over at the coin shop in Bigtown. They're stalling him till we get there. Want to press charges and have him arrested?"

"Any idea who he is?" the Preacher asked.

"Says his name's Theo Casey from right here in Tinyburg."

Taking a deep breath and biting his lip to see if he were dreaming, the Preacher replied, "I'll go over myself, but don't arrest him."

At first, Theo was defensive, protesting he didn't understand all the fuss. Still in shock from disbelief the Preacher promised that if Theo would meet him that night, they'd forget the police for now.

After supper, in the church office, Theo argued that all he'd tried to do was sell a couple of coins he'd gotten in change, maybe at the bank. "What am I being accused of?" he asked. "I don't even know where I got them—I just recognized they were bound to have some value. And here you called the police, as if I were a criminal or something."

"Theo, you know where those coins came from," the Preacher replied. "They came out of the offering plates, by someone, somehow. And you're the only man in the church, besides the counting committee, that has access to the church safe. Frankly, it looks suspicious."

Theo's face reddened. His eyes fell to the floor, his lips

quivered, his shoulders drooped. "Preacher, I'm gonna level with you. I could lie my way out of this. But I'm not. Yes, I took those coins out of the safe before the committee arrived. In fact, for several months, I've been going back to the church, right after dinner, and taking about $15 in bills and coins. Not enough to be missed, but enough for my needs."

"What do you mean your *needs*?" the Preacher asked, with sarcasm in his voice. "You make a good salary; why would you steal a paltry fifteen dollars a week?"

"Years ago," Theo explained, "a man here in Tinyburg hired me and another fellow to work at his mill. That's before I studied accounting. I worked hard—lots harder than the other employee. But he was always buttering up the boss, doing little favors for him, and the boss was naive enough to swallow it. When he got a fifteen-dollar a week raise and I didn't, I swore someday to get even."

"Well, my old boss is a member of this church, although he's now in a nursing home. As treasurer, I knew his family still sent about $15 a week as his offering. I decided that $15 was mine. So I've been taking it."

The Preacher shook his head in disbelief. "Theo, I wouldn't have been hurt more if one of my own teenage sons were caught stealing. But you, a grown man, financially secure, prominent in the church, and my own good fishing and golfing buddy . . . man, I'm hurt. I'm crushed.

"It's not that I'm just disappointed in you, but in myself, my whole ministry. If I've failed with you, I've evidently failed lots of others here in Tinyburg. Maybe my whole ministry's just a farce, a make-believe. You make me feel like throwing my Bible in the trash and never entering a pulpit again."

"Preacher, I don't blame you for feeling that way. In my head, I knew it was wrong, all along. But I guess my heart made me do it. That old desire for revenge got the best of me. I know there's nothing I can say to make you believe in me again. I'll resign as treasurer, make good the deficit, just drop out of sight. You'll never be embarrassed by me again."

As word spread, some members wanted to press charges and have Theo indicted. Others said that so long as he paid it all back, the less said the better. But after Clay Barker, president of Tinyburg Realty, remarked in the men's Bible class that more than money was involved here—a matter of principle and setting an example for the youth—that it was decided to air the matter in an open business session.

Uncle Billy Cutrell was the first to speak: "I've been telling you folks there's a little clique runnin' this church. If we'd passed these jobs around, not let one man serve as treasurer so long, he wouldn't have had all this temptation."

Right about then, to the surprise of everyone, Theo Casey walked in and asked to speak. "I just want to say three things," he began, looking at the floor. "First, to resign as treasurer. Second, to confess my sin and ask you to take my name off the roll. And third, since we don't have a custodian right now, to say that I'd like to work out what I owe. Maybe it'll help my conscience. Oh, I could write a check for the whole amount. But maybe if I washed windows a few months, mowed the grass this summer, got my hands in Lysol water cleaning the rest rooms, I'd feel better."

A long silence followed, for that's not exactly what the folks expected to hear. Then the Preacher, speaking so softly that some had to strain to hear, reminded them of the prodigal son, told in Luke 15.

"When the prodigal came to himself, he realized his father's hired servants had more to eat than he did. So he resolved to go home, not to ask reinstatement as a son, but for a job as a servant or slave. Instead, his father threw his arms around him, loved him, forgave him, killed a fatted calf, put new shoes on his feet, and a new ring on his finger.

"Theo's not asking to be a member anymore, just a hired hand, sweeping floors." Then he sat down, sobbing. For the first time in his ministry he was unable to control his feelings.

After a long silence, Uncle Billy said, "If I'm in order, I want to make three motions: First, to accept his resignation as treasurer. Second, not to erase his name from the roll. And third, to hire him as custodian until he works out what he took." Without waiting for a second or a call for the vote, nearly everyone shouted "Amen" in unison.

With that, the Preacher walked back to Theo, put his arms around him, and for a long minute the two stood there, both weeping, both trembling with emotion. On an impulse, the organist started playing, "Amazing grace! how sweet the sound, That saved a wretch like me! . . ." One by one, others in the congregation followed, until only Clay Barker was left. "Don't act like a baby, Clay," his wife whispered, and with a bold step he reached for Theo, and the two hugged as if each were trying to choke the other.

"I'll start tomorrow," Theo promised. "Sunday's Easter, and that'll give me three days to make this old church shine."

Thursday, he washed every window, inside and out.

Friday, he scrubbed and waxed all the halls and class-room floors, dusted the pews, vacuumed the carpets, and cleaned the rest rooms until the fixtures shone like new.

On Saturday, he made the rounds of florists and variety stores, not only in Tinyburg but also Bigtown, buying pots of blooming flowers—lilies, hyacinths, tulips, daffodils, and narcissus. Loading them in his pickup, he delivered them to the church, then lined the sidewalk with them. He knew the interior would spill over with Easter flowers, but he wanted to decorate his own triumphal entry, his own Via Dolorosa, to the church that meant so much to him.

Easter dawned bright and sunny, and more than one member—especially some of the elderly who had been shut in most of the winter—felt a lump in their throats when they saw the churchyard ablaze with color.

Sunday afternoon, Theo loaded the potted plants and delivered them to the Tinyburg Nursing Home. Fortunately, there was one for each room.

In the last room lay Theo's boss, motionless and unspeaking after a recent stroke. Saying nothing, Theo placed the flowers near his bed . . . hesitated . . . then bent over and kissed his forehead. Then he reached for the old man's hand, held it tightly, and to his surprise, felt a grip in response.

Whether the old man knew, Theo didn't know. One thing he did know, that whereas he was lost, now he was found, and that this was an Easter of all Easters to remember.

Christmas Is for Lovers

For twenty-nine Decembers, Candice Carpenter had directed the Christmas plays at the Tinyburg Church. Candice, who always loved the stage, once dreamed of a master's degree in theater. Instead, she dropped out of college at the end of her freshman year and married her high-school sweetheart, Ted Carpenter.

Back then, few women combined a career with marriage, so Candice chose Ted over the theater. She and Ted shared a good life in Tinyburg, living just two streets over from her parents, Mr. and Mrs. Clay Barker.

Ted, an abstracter at the courthouse, sometimes helped his father-in-law with auctions and estate sales.

Candice busied herself with raising a family, pouring into the annual Christmas play all her pent-up enthusiasm for acting and theatrics. Not one to put off until the last minute, she always started soon after Labor Day assigning parts, making costumes and holding rehearsals.

Of special appeal was Candice's use of live animals in her plays. Without exception, she managed to round up at least one sheep, a lamb, a calf, or a donkey.

One Christmas the script called for a live camel. Candice had no idea where she could borrow a camel, until fortune smiled on her efforts in early December.

A small circus, enroute to Florida for the winter, suffered a major equipment breakdown near Bigtown. Since repair parts were slow in coming, the show people were held up for about two weeks.

As soon as Candice read the story in the *Tinyburg News,* she drove over to Bigtown and persuaded the animal trainer to loan her a camel by the name of Rosie.

The trainer agreed, with the understanding that he would come along to look after Rosie, and that Rosie could appear only the night of the performance. "I can't bring Rosie to the rehearsals—just the night of the play," he explained.

When word spread that a real, live camel by the name of Rosie would be in Candice's Christmas play, the church sure enough couldn't hold the folks.

At first, everything went OK. Led by her trainer, Rosie walked up the front steps. However, upon reaching the door, she balked.

Her trainer begged, pleaded, scolded, and threatened. He pushed awhile, then pulled. But Rosie wouldn't budge. He ordered her to kneel, so her long neck and humps would go through the door. But Rosie held her ground, her head high. Some who were sitting on the back row near the door said they heard profanity, right there on the church steps.

I understand that after this, the circus billed Rosie as "the camel who wouldn't go to church." That may be hearsay. I never read such ads myself.

Although everyone was disappointed, the show went on while Rosie retreated to Bigtown. "Next year it'll be an elephant!" observed Uncle Billy Told-You-So. "Or a rhinoceros or hippopotamus, who knows?"

As the popularity of Candice's plays grew through the

years, the crowds required two performances. Folks from other churches usually came on Saturday night, and members for the most part attended the Sunday-night performance.

And after each New Year's was over, she cooked and hosted a big dinner at her home for the cast. Her sole helper was Mary, twenty-eight, a mildly retarded young woman with a speech impediment, who did shampoos at the Tinyburg Beauty Shop.

Mary helped mainly with the costumes, laundering and pressing them, putting them on hangers between rehearsals, then folding and packing them away for next year.

For the thirtieth annual performance Candice took unusual care in choosing a suitable play, finally decided on "No Greater Love." That same fall, the old Tinyburg High School consolidated with a new unit school, and youngsters were bussed in from all over. New courses were offered in speech, playwriting, and drama.

The school board hired Sam Belford, who had three summers of experience in summer-stock theater, to teach the new courses. Sam, with a master's degree in theater, was an instant success. Young, talented, handsome, and single—there was a waiting list for his classes.

When Candice met Sam at an open house for the new school, some of her old dreams sprang to life. She remembered the excitement of her one year of college and, momentarily, questioned whether she had made the right choices.

Then on an impulse she asked Sam, "I don't guess you'd help direct our church Christmas play?"

To her surprise, Sam agreed, saying he'd been wanting a chance for community involvement, to meet some of the adults as well as younger children in Tinyburg.

Candice was pleased at the response of the members. With Sam as codirector, more people than ever showed up for tryouts, more offered to make costumes and design props, and volunteers even started bringing refreshments to rehearsals and chauffering kids who needed rides home after dark. And it seemed to Candice that every teenage girl in town wanted to do something, even putting up posters or passing out programs.

As enthusiasm mounted Candice was not only pleased, but a mite overwhelmed. However, these feelings gradually turned inward on her, as she speculated why in other years she hadn't enjoyed such cooperation . . . why Mary was the only dependable help she ever had.

Still, she was able to announce at the first dress rehearsal—with all sincerity—"Why, this is going to be the best play I've ever had anything to do with!"

And then it happened, as it often does when someone means to compliment but instead hurts, and hurts deeply. To this day, Candice can't remember who said it. The following words cut so deeply into her heart that they erased all memory of who spoke them:

"Yes, Candice, the best play of all, because this year we have *a real professional* for a director!"

Candice, caught off guard, was stunned. "Professional . . . professional . . . professional . . . " The word echoed and reverberated, as if amplified with a public-address system and burned into her mind like a cattle brand on the flanks of a steer.

Then the dam burst and thirty years of pent-up disappointment suddenly broke loose. Turning to the startled cast and helpers and parents, and with tears streaking her face, she almost screamed:

"Professional? You don't know a professional when you see one. Half of you couldn't spell the word if your life depended on it. I'm a professional, too, in case you don't know it. I studied drama in college, read everything I could get on the subject, went to workshops, then drilled, drilled, and drilled the likes of you for twenty-nine years!

"Oh, I realize a forty-nine-year-old housewife doesn't sweep you off your feet like a twenty-three-year-old bachelor, fresh from summer stock. But where were you those years I needed help in making costumes, borrowing spotlights, picking up kids, wrangling money out of the finance committee to pay authors' royalties, mimeographing programs the night before the performance, wiping noses of disappointed kids who tried out but couldn't make it? Tell me, if you're so brilliant, and know all about professionals!"

As Candice paused to catch her breath, two little angel-children, wearing white robes and wings, started to cry.

"It won't do any good to sniffle," Candice snapped at them. "You don't know what hurt is. Wait 'til you've given your best for thirty years, without a thank you, and then you can cry."

The whole scene was unreal. Those who were there, and recall it, say it was like they were dreaming.

Candice felt the same way. It was as if she were hearing a recording of her own voice, repeating things she didn't want to say but couldn't keep from saying. She felt disembodied, like a spectator to all she was hearing. She wanted to stop the recording—if that's what it was. But she was powerless. The words continued in torrents . . .

"I guess after New Year's, Sam will invite you all over at his place for a big dinner. Think he can crowd you all into his tiny apartment? Maybe he can send out for hamburgers and fries, since he's such a professional.

"I've sewed enough fragile angel wings to outfit Gabriel's choir, burned my hands on footlights, picked up enough bathrobes at Goodwill to clothe all the shepherds in Galilee, cut shepherd staffs out of cardboard until I wore blisters on my hands, rehearsed and rehearsed until even the beautiful lines from Luke's Gospel jarred my nerves and left me sleepless, made enough treasure chests for Wise Men to empty the button boxes of all the grandmas in Tinyburg, popped enough corn for treats to fill the Tinyburg swimming pool . . . "

Desperately, now, Candice longed to stop the torrent, but like someone fumbling in the dark with an unfamiliar tape recorder, she couldn't find the "off" button.

"You're a nice lot to talk about professionals. If you were members of any of the churches over in Bigtown, you couldn't even pass an audition to hand out programs.

"To be honest, I'll tell you exactly what you are. All of you. You're a bunch of small-town hicks. The only stage you qualify for is here in the Tinyburg Church. And let me remind you, that isn't Broadway—not even close.

"My only regret is that I wasted twenty-nine Christmases on you, Christmases I could have given my family. Well, this is one I'm really going to enjoy, so let your professional there take over.

"He'll discover what I've known all along, and that is you're all a bunch of amateurs. And from now on, I'm not going to waste my time on amateurs, clods with no appreciation for a person with real talent."

With that, she picked up her coat and on the way out,

slammed the door so hard that a framed picture of Jesus, blessing the children, fell to the floor and shattered.

Candice left behind her not only a stunned cast, but also a church filled with silence. Finally, Sam broke the spell.

"Folks, I never dreamed anything like this would happen when I agreed to help," he apologized. "I wouldn't have gotten mixed up in this for the world.

"However, as surprising as this may be, I agree with Candice. All of you—each of you—is an amateur. But let me explain. Our English word *amateur* comes from the Latin *amat*, meaning to love. An amateur is not someone who's paid or even qualified. An amateur acts out of love, because he wants to.

"That's what's so great about mothers! They're all amateurs in the nicest sense of the word.

"One other thing—I can't believe that was Candice Carpenter up there tonight, talking like that. But to be a professional actor, one must feel deeply and then learn to surface those emotions. Candice feels deeply about life. And she let it all come out. Some folks keep their feelings bottled up for a lifetime. They never cry, deep down in their gut. Neither do they laugh, a real belly kind of laughing."

As Candice pulled into the drive, she took heart that Ted was away, deer hunting. She could never explain her reddened eyes, her splitting headache. Finally, after three aspirins, she fell asleep.

The next morning was her weekly appointment at the Tinyburg Beauty Shop. Her first thought was not to go, fearful of whom she might see, but she did anyway.

Mary met her at the door, her face glowing with excitement. "Oh, Mis Carpter," she said, slowly forming her words which never seemed to come out properly. "Mis Carpter, I an anater, I an anater, I an a real anater!"

Candice, accustomed to Mary's speech pattern, easily followed her explanation:

"Sam sed we al' anaters, cuz we luv what we du, ev'n if we don' not have eny ed-cay-shun. All us anaters."

Candice was a proud woman, ambitious, hard-working, determined, self-disciplined, and, to some, apparently self-sufficient—but never blind to her own faults. As Mary repeated Sam's words, she clearly and quickly saw herself, as if in a mirror.

The same afternoon she was waiting in the hallway of the new school, when Sam's last class dismissed.

"Sam," she began. "I've done a lot of silly things in my life, but last night topped them all. You may not believe me when I say I'm sorry, but I am. And I want you to finish the play. I can't go back. But I'll be on the front row, Christmas Eve, when the curtain goes up. Be a good trooper, Sam, and make it possible for that curtain to go up."

"I will," he whispered.

From then until Christmas, Mary was at Candice's house every night. Neighbors and friends speculated, but asked no questions. It was not like Candice to stay so close at home.

As she promised, Candice was on the front row when the curtains parted for "No Greater Love." Ted sat on one side, Mary on the other. The house was full, the performance flawless, the music as tender as a baby's smile.

At the conclusion, Candice asked to say a word. "By now, all of you know what happened a few nights ago. I'm not here to resurrect that scenario. I *am* here to present a gift to each family, on behalf of Mary and myself."

With that signal, Ted came down front with two big boxes. They were filled with silver balls, the kind most people in Tinyburg decorate their trees with.

Only these were different. On each silver ball were four hand-lettered words, "Christmas is for lovers."

"I painted these," Candice explained, "and Mary sprinkled them with glitter, while the paint was still wet. Of course we're just amateurs, but that's what Christmas is all about.

"That's why so-called professionals often miss the soul of Christmas."

The next day, Christmas trees all over Tinyburg were festooned with the silvery ornaments, each sharing its message in red lettering, sprinkled with silver glitter.

I understand that with the passing of the years, these ornaments are beginning to be handed down to the next generation, prized far beyond their material value.

If you can't visit Tinyburg around Christmas, stop by anytime at the home of Uncle Billy Cutrell, who lives across the street from the church. He never packs away his silver ball, but keeps it handy for anyone who likes to be reminded—even in mid-July—that Christmas is for lovers.

The Pin Oak Tree

One of the first things the Preacher and his wife did when they moved to Tinyburg was to set out a pin oak tree in their backyard.

"One of the nicest trees you can plant," the nurseryman advised. "Yes, they're slow growing, especially the first couple of years. But once a pin oak's rooted, it really takes off."

Counting the time they set it out, that pin oak was moved three times. Twice it was relocated—when the trustees added a family room to the pastorium and two years later enlarged the garage.

After six years, it was still about the same size. "Be patient," the Preacher told his family one afternoon. "If we don't wear that tree out moving it around, we may live to see it big enough to hold a bird's nest or two." That night, Rev. Henry Moss, D.D., called from Bigtown.

"Say, Preacher," Dr. Moss began. "Know that new church over in Growth Unlimited? They've asked me for a recommendation, and I want to give them your name. My, what you could do there. New industries. Rows and rows of new homes. Young couples with growing families. Not a lot of old deadwood to put up with."

The Preacher asked Henry for time to think it over. Just a few days earlier, he'd come home depressed from a

133

three-day seminar in Dr. Moss's church. Moss held these annually, so other ministers could learn the latest in church growth.

"The way I see it, our city churches are the hope of our nation," Dr. Moss had told the clinicians, most of them from small towns like Tinyburg. "Here we are at the crossroads, where the multitudes pour in from the countryside. It's in the cities where key decisions are made that influence all of America.

"Take Bigtown. Right down the street from our church is one of the great medical schools and teaching hospitals in the land. Each Sunday as I stand in my pulpit, I'm awed by the business and professional people who flock to hear me. Leaders in medicine, government, science— you name it, we have it.

"Brethren I can't tell you the responsibility I feel. It sobers me when I think of the rippling effect of my sermons. Like ocean waves, they touch distant shores unseen by me."

Driving home from that seminar, a sinking feeling hit the Preacher's stomach when he reached the sign that read, Tinyburg: 5 miles. *A better name would be Jumping-off Place,* he had muttered to himself.

Now all was about to change. Already he could see himself in the pulpit at "Growth Unlimited."

It was August, and after Dr. Moss hung up, the Preacher went outside, alone. He couldn't keep his eyes off the pin oak which for six years had struggled valiantly. Each time, a move had set it back. He thought of Psalm 1:3, "And he shall be like a tree planted by the rivers of water, that bringeth forth his fruit . . . "

He recalled the friends they had made in Tinyburg,

the roots his children had put down, the dreams not yet realized.

Dr. Moss was visibly upset the next morning when the Preacher called to say he was staying in Tinyburg. "You don't mean you're going to stay—you mean you're going to rot," he warned. "You can't imagine how this will cripple your future. At Growth Unlimited, you might have your own television show."

"I appreciate your concern," the Preacher interrupted, "but my mind's made up."

"OK, just stay there and be a one-horse, one-gallus, jackleg preacher," Dr. Moss replied in a veiled sarcasm. "Five years from now you'll be lucky if attendance is what it is today. Face it, man, Tinyburg's a has-been. And pardon me for saying it, but all this pious talk about 'suffering for Jesus' won't put bread on your table. If I'm a child of the King, why should I eat at a pig trough? And pardon me again, but Tinyburg's not far ahead of a pig's trough."

The years passed. The pin oak grew. The leaves wore light-green jackets in the spring and brilliant sweaters in the fall. The birds nested. As it grew, the Preacher made a swing for his toddlers. As youngsters, they played house under its foliage. As youth, they climbed its sturdy branches. As a family, they enjoyed summer cookouts under its shade.

Years later, the Preacher ran into Dr. Moss at a national convention. "How's the attendance holding up in Tinyburg?" Dr. Moss wanted to know. "Oh, about the same," the Preacher replied. "Maybe even down a little. The last census showed we lost 180 in population. But a work crew from our church just got back from overseas.

They helped build a mission chapel. Our church paid for everything—their travel, building materials, even furnishings.

"And myself, I'm busier than ever. The longer I stay in Tinyburg, the more folks seem to trust me. My counseling has doubled, maybe tripled. Not just our members, but folks from other faiths. They sometimes bring me problems they wouldn't dare tell their own pastor, saying it's because they know me so well. 'Course I'm not a magician. I can't patch every torn place in folks' hearts. But I've mended enough to make me feel good, deep inside.

"And lots of summer mornings, after breakfast, I take my coffee, Bible, and notebook and sit under that big pin oak tree in our backyard. And I just let the Lord speak to me. You'd be surprised the sermons I get out there, ones I never find in commentaries and Bible encyclopedias.

"And Dr. Moss, you can say I'm sentimental, but when the Lord God finished the Garden, well, he planted all kinds of trees, especially the Tree of Life . . . and brother, I've found my life, I've found my tree!"

The last time I was in Tinyburg, I drove by the parsonage (whatever you care to call it) and that pin oak's bigger than ever. Be worth your time to drive over and see it for yourself, especially some bright day in October.

The New White Suit

It's not that Clay Barker and S. Franklin Rodd were enemies. Just not what you'd call close friends. Maybe because they were so much alike, especially in their dress.

Clay, president of Tinyburg Realty, is the only man in town who wears a coat and tie 365 days in the year. If you see him at the July 4 picnic, he'll have on a tie, sporting a celluloid doodad in his breast coat pocket. That's to hold an assortment of pencils, fountain pens, and ball-point pens.

"Never know when you'll close a deal," he often explained, "and I want to be ready to sign on the dotted line."

Frank Rodd also went dressed up most of the time, but impeccably so. In contrast to Clay, who was short and portly and rumpled-like in appearance, Frank was tall, thin, and immaculate.

His snow-white hair and matching, close-cropped mustache gave him almost a patrician bearing. He wore spats in winter and year round carried a gold-tipped cane.

Frank was what folks in Tinyburg called a gentleman farmer. He lived on a large acreage, about three miles from town, which he inherited from his grandfather. He raised a few cattle, then rented out the rest of the land,

137

which gave him and Mrs. Rodd a comfortable income. His neat, white farmhouse with its green shutters, surrounded by a picket fence and lawn as closely cropped as his mustache, fitted his personality.

Clay was not long from retirement when out of a clear blue sky he announced to Mrs. Barker that he was going to run for county tax assessor. When she tried to discourage him, pointing out he'd never run for anything in his life and that now was the time to enjoy their retirement years, Clay replied, "But for once, I want to see 'Clay Barker' engraved on one of the courthouse office doors."

The election was close, for both men had lots of friends, but Clay lost. Talk around the courthouse was that too many voters feared a conflict of interest, having a realtor as assessor. "With the property he owns plus buying and selling all the time, he might be tempted to tamper with some of the assessments," one observer noted.

Clay, always a big joker, now made Frank the object of what some felt was a raw, caustic humor. His lifelong friends knew that Clay Barker was flamboyant. But cynical, no. At least not until he lost the election.

But what really riled Clay Barker was the first set of tax bills that came after the election. When he totaled the increases, he was sure S. Frank Rodd was getting some kind of revenge.

"Now that Frank's assessor, has gotten both feet in the feed trough down at the courthouse, he's got uppity, biggety," Clay remarked at the Tinyburg Cafe one morning. "Won't even say 'howdy-do' anymore. I always wondered what that *S* stood for in front of his name. Now I know. It stands for sashayin', because he's always

sashayin' around somewhere, his head up in the air.
There he goes now—Sashayin' Frank Rodd."

"And if there's anything I don't like," Clay continued,
raising his voice so everyone could hear, "it's a sissy man
or a prissy woman. Well, when the good Lord made S.
Franklin Rodd, he stirred both ingredients in the same
mixin' bowl. He's a sissy, prissy, dapper dude."

"Why don't you lay off?" interrupted Uncle Billy
Cutrell, there for his usual morning coffee. "You're
hurting yourself more than the assessor. It's not like you,
Clay."

"I'm not out to hurt anybody—just telling the truth.
And the truth is that 'Ramrod' Rodd doesn't fit the
Tinyburg mold. You know it, and I know it. And if I'm
the only man in town with enough courage to tell it like it
is, then so be it."

That was the first time anyone heard Clay use the
nickname "Ramrod," but it wasn't the last.

The next Saturday afternoon, as usual, Clay Barker
closed the downstairs offices of his agency and walked
upstairs to his private office. It overlooked Main Street,
and he enjoyed sitting up there, watching the folks go by.

In the summer, he opened the window and leaned back
in a cane-bottom chair, his feet propped up on the sill.
"When I was a boy," Clay often recalled, "farmers would
come to town on Saturdays, leave their wagons at the
hitching rack, then do their tradin', exchanging eggs and
butter and the like for sugar and flour and dry goods. I
like to sit up here and imagine some of those good ole
farm folks are still walkin' down Main Street."

Only this Saturday afternoon, Clay was preoccupied
with S. Franklin Rodd, not nostalgia.

About that time he spied Frank coming down the

sidewalk. On an impulse, and without really thinking, Clay leaned out the window and cried out loud enough for anyone to hear, "Hey, there, Ramrod, how about sellin' you a piece of elastic for that backbone?"

As usual, Frank said nothing, looking neither to the right or the left nor to the upstairs window. But with head erect, his gold-tipped cane making staccato echoes on the concrete walk, he kept going.

Breathing a sigh of self-satisfaction, Clay leaned back, smugly reminding himself that S. Franklin Rodd was indeed a sissy man. Else he wouldn't take remarks like that.

But for once, Clay misjudged Frank; for when he reached the corner, he turned right and came back up the alley. Knowing a back door to Clay's offices opened from the alley, Frank quietly let himself in. Then taking off his shoes, he tiptoed up the steps in his stocking feet.

As Frank entered the upstairs office, Clay's back was now to him, still watching the passersby. Cautiously, he tiptoed to where Clay was sitting, tilted back in his cane-bottomed chair. Then, with a lunge, he seized him by the shoulders, crying "Man overboard! Man overboard!" as loud as he could. And with the same motion, he gave Clay a shove as if to push him out the window.

Clay was so taken aback, as well as frightened, that Frank was down the stairs and gone before Clay could see who he was. But he had a good idea it was Frank's voice, a suspicion confirmed by a couple of boys playing marbles in the alley.

The next morning, getting ready for church, Clay had trouble knotting his tie. Tuesday morning, signing some deeds at the courthouse, he thought his hand trembled more than usual.

What began as a trickle became a stream. Three weeks later he made an appointment with Dr. G. S. Gordon. "Don't know what's wrong, Doc," he began, "but I seem to have the tremblies. Been taking nerve tablets, but don't seem to do me no good."

"When did you first notice it?" Dr. Gordon asked. "Oh, maybe three weeks ago. Came on real gradual-like."

Dr. Gordon told Clay it looked like the shaking palsy. "Could be a symptom of Parkinson's disease," the doctor added. "Anything bothering you? Upset? Worried? Had any sudden shocks?"

Then, for the first time, he told how Frank Rodd had slipped up and scared him, making him think he was being pushed out of an upstairs window.

"Do you think Frank Rodd could be to blame for all this, and that I might end up a tremblin', shakin' invalid?" Clay asked in a tone of voice as if he didn't really want an answer.

"I don't think anybody could prove it, one way or another," Dr. Gordon replied. "It's possible you've had a mild case of Parkinson's disease a long time, and just now started to notice it."

In the weeks ahead, as his trembling hands and arms worsened, so did his feelings toward Frank. That's when he decided to see an attorney. In a matter of days, he had filed a lawsuit against Frank Rodd, asking for $10,000 in damages, a big sum back then.

Six months later, the case came to a jury trial, in some respects more like a circus than anything. The townspeople were fascinated with the testimony, especially the report of Clay calling Frank a sissy, prissy, dapper dude.

When the foreman of the jury announced they had found Frank Rodd guilty, he explained how they reasoned. "Some contend the palsy was comin' on Clay anyway," he said. "But we figured that's about like saying that if someone shot a fellow, who knows, he might have died of a heart attack anyway."

When the time came for sentencing, the judge asked both men to stand before him. "I've known you fellows for a long time," he began. "Both of you are good men— one of you an elected official, the other a respected businessman. Although you're not members of the same church, both of you are Christian leaders. You're respectable men, not the kind of people I ordinarily see in these chambers.

"The truth is, both of you are guilty. Guilty of acting like schoolboys, instead of grown men. The sentence: one dollar in cash, payable to the plaintiff before you leave this courtroom."

Both men left without speaking, each feeling vindicated, not realizing that each had also lost.

Clay framed the dollar bill, hanging it in a prominent place in his office, joking about it to his clients.

The morning after the verdict, Clay Barker called the best sign painter in Bigtown. "Come over and bring some bright orange paint," he added.

When the painter arrived, Clay asked him to scrape off the lettering on the plate-glass window downstairs. The old copy had read "Tinyburg Realty Company" in big letters, arranged in a half circle. Underneath, in smaller lettering were the words, "Clay Barker, President."

"I want the sign reversed," Clay told the painter. "Put my name in big letters. Then at the bottom, in smaller letters, the name of my company."

"But Mr. Barker," the painter complained, "I don't think that's going to look right. You always put the name of the firm in big letters. And this bright orange paint is going to make it look like a circus poster."

"I don't care what you think," Clay shot back. "It's my name, my company, my window, and my money."

And so it was done. And for days afterward, traffic on Main Street often came to a sudden stop when a motorist slowed down in disbelief at what he saw on Clay's window. "Clay Barker's Rainbow" is what Fred "Fixit" Turner quickly dubbed it, and everyone picked up on the joke. So it became common to refer to Clay's business as "The Rainbow Office."

Two weeks later, it was Clay's turn to serve communion at the Tinyburg Church. Mrs. Barker tried to dissuade him. "Clay, trembly as you are, what'd happen if you spilled some of the glasses?"

But Clay, who took pride in helping to prepare and serve the elements, said one more time wouldn't hurt, and he'd be extra careful.

On the same Sunday, Frank Rodd decided to visit the Tinyburg Church, since his grandson was singing in the youth choir. Ordinarily, he and Mrs. Rodd attended a little church about five miles out in the country.

Neither had spoken to each other since the trial. In fact, Clay didn't even know Frank was present until it was his turn to pass the cups on the side where Frank was sitting, next to the aisle.

Frank looked unusually dapper, wearing a new, white linen suit, an eggshell silk tie, and a yellow rosebud in his lapel.

Whether it was shock at seeing Frank or the normal twitching of his hands, Clay never knew. He just knows that as he reached Frank's pew, he dropped the tray, and the tiny glasses of grape juice spilled all down the front of

Frank's white linen coat and trousers, silk tie, and yellow rosebud.

The only sound was a loud gasp from Aunt Sarah Biggs, sitting on the front row of the choir. But her gasp was so shrill that the organist, fearing at worst she had suffered a stroke—or at best had swallowed a bug—stopped playing momentarily. A long silence gripped the congregation, relieved only by the giggling of some children.

"Let's stand for the benediction," announced the Preacher knowing the service was beyond recovery.

Clay Barker, now as solicitous and apologetic as he had been caustic and cynical, escorted Frank to a side room; he helped him to change into one of the white jump suits that the church kept on hand for baptizings.

"Frank, you've got every reason to believe that was deliberate," Clay began. "But believe me, it was an accident. I've not only acted like a fool—I've been one. I got carried away, wanting to see my name on the courthouse door. Now my name's dirt, sure enough. I'll never live this down . . . "

"Now let me tell you a thing or two," interrupted Frank, zipping up his jump suit. "I haven't exactly acted like an adult myself. And if you're worried about this suit, let me tell you about my first trip to the county fair. Guess I was about six years old, all dressed up in a new sailor suit with a big white collar and short, white pants. First thing off, I spilled a grape snow cone all down the front. I cringed, sure that Mother would swat me, right there in front of everybody. And do you know what she said? She was the sweetest mother a boy ever had, and I can still hear her saying, 'That's all right Frankie, the world's full of sailor suits.' And with that she laughed, dried me off, and bought me another snow cone!"

When it was announced that communion was re-scheduled for the following Sunday, Frank and his wife decided to visit again. And if you'd seen them sitting on the same pew with Mr. and Mrs. Clay Barker, you'd have sworn they were bosom pals from childhood.

In his message the Preacher referred, good-naturedly, to the preceding Sunday. Then he added, "Spilling the wine last Sunday may have been more symbolical than drinking it this Sunday. For that's what happened at Calvary. There, Jesus spilled his blood, and by his stripes we are healed."

In closing they sang:

> **There is a fountain filled with blood**
> **Drawn from Immanuel's veins;**
> **And sinners, plunged beneath that flood,**
> **Lose all their guilty stains.**

—WILLIAM COWPER

Should you decide to drive over to Tinyburg to meet Frank and Clay, the best time is on a Saturday afternoon.

In the summertime, especially, you'll find them sitting with their feet propped up on the windowsill in Clay's office, watching the country folk do their tradin'.

And if you run into Dr. Gordon, ask him how his practice is doing. He'll probably say that if all his patients recovered as quickly as Clay Barker, he'd have to take down his shingle and look for another job.

Susan's Doll

The Preacher at Tinyburg Church probably conducted more funerals than any minister in town. He was popular with the unchurched as well. And if a family had no choice, or a stranger was brought back for burial, the mortician called him. "You know, Preacher, I've heard a lot of eulogies," the mortician confided in him one day, "but you give the mourners something to live for. And you fit each service to the situation. Would you believe one minister repeated the same message at a two o'clock funeral that he'd given at another the same morning? One was for a seventy-eight-year-old man, and the other for a ten-month-old baby. Same illustrations, same poetry, same everything."

But burying the dead was the last thing on the Preacher's mind that August morning when he left to serve as a counselor at a youth camp. As he passed the bedroom where his oldest son, Mark, was still asleep, he noticed how the early morning sunlight flickered on his face.

In a few days, Mark would be leaving for his freshman year in college, and a sudden lump rose in the Preacher's throat. He loved all three of his sons, but there was something special about Mark. Maybe it was his outgoing nature, always helping someone.

In fact, the Preacher often scolded Mark for being too trusting. He remembered Mark's first day in school when he gave his lunch to a new friend. "But Dad, that's what you preach," is how Mark defended himself.

The Preacher enjoyed camp, but by Thursday night he could hardly wait for Friday, so he could go home.

He was still awake when the camp director roused him with an urgent call.

"Preacher, this is the sheriff back in Tinyburg," an ominous and far-off voice began. "I'm sorry to call this time of night and, well, Preacher, I just don't know how to say it and . . . "

"Go on," he replied tensely.

"You know your son, Mark, well, there's been a bad accident, and well, uh, Preacher, I'm sorry as I can be, but Mark's not with us anymore . . . "

"You mean, you mean, he's . . . dead?" the Preacher whispered in disbelief.

"'Fraid so. You see, a bad thunderstorm hit here about dark. Mark stopped at the top of a hill to help an elderly couple change a tire. The right-of-way was muddy, and they didn't pull off like they should. And while Mark was changing the tire in the rain, well, another car sideswiped him . . . "

Everyone admired the Preacher's composure at the visitation and the memorial service. Comforting his distraught wife and Mark's brothers was his chief concern. "Here's a man with real faith," whispered Uncle Billy Cutrell at the funeral home. "He's an example for us. Instead of breaking down, he's got a hold of himself for the sake of his family."

And so life returned to normal in the pastorium, the church, and about town . . . as normal as possible after you've buried a seventeen-year-old kid liked by everyone.

But as fall approached and the days shortened, grow-ing shorter still in December, the winter's darkness drove the Preacher into deep depression. No one knew, for he was a good actor.

To console himself in private, he often leafed through sermon notes, poems, and Scriptures he quoted at funer-als:

> I am the resurrection, and the life: he that believeth in me, though he were dead, yet shall he live (John 11:25).

But such words only mocked him. It seemed as if a devilish imp were sitting on his shoulder, mocking his faith, whispering doubts in his ears.

He scanned "In Memory of a Child" by Vachel Lindsay:

> The angels guide him now
> And watch his curly head,
> And lead him in their games,
>   The little boy we led.
>
> He cannot come to harm,
> He knows more than we know,
>   His light is brighter far
> Than daytime here below.
>
> His path leads on and on,
> Through pleasant lawns and flowers,
>   His brown eyes open wide
> At grass more green than ours.
>
>   With playmates like himself,
>   The shining boy will sing,
>   Exploring wondrous woods,
>   Sweet with eternal spring.

But although these words had comforted other parents, they sounded empty and hollow to him. He felt like a hypocrite.

Winter crept slowly, but it passed, and spring touched the hillsides around Tinyburg, turning them green with hope as if wakened by a magic wand.

It was a wet spring, the ground sodden and water-logged. So it was no surprise when a Good Friday mini-cloudburst flooded some low-lying homes. Saturday morning, the Preacher took a load of warm clothing and food to the refugees, housed in the high school gym. Some residents had lost everything.

The first person he met was Susan, age five. "Hi, Preacher," she said with a big smile. "Guess what? I've still got Dolly, my favorite doll. Look!"

And with that she held up a miserably wet rag of a doll with stringy hair and sodden clothes.

Driving home, the Preacher couldn't forget her words, "Look! I've still got Dolly!" The next morning, he laid aside his carefully prepared Easter message.

"Friends, for months you've talked about how strong I am. But that's a lie. Inside, I'm broken, defeated. Oh, I mouthed the words, but the pain was still there. The doubts smothered me. My grief is raw. I've found no balm of Gilead. The Good Shepherd has not taken my hand."

Stopping to tell about Susan's doll, he then continued, "Too long, I've majored on what we lost, and we did lose a lot when we buried Mark. But starting today, like Susan, I'm going to major on what's left.

"Why, I have a lovely wife, two boys, other relatives, and you, my fellow Christian friends. I have good health, faith in the resurrection, and the ultimate triumph of

good. But in spite of all this, I was too proud to let you
see me cry. Yes, I believe. But like Thomas of old, I need
help with my unbelief, too."

At this point, he just stood there. And if you think
there's silence in heaven as described in Revelation 8:1,
you should have heard the silence of that Easter congregation.

And although he knew Lindsay's poem described a
younger boy, he closed by reading:

> The angels guide him now,
> And watch his curly head.
> And lead him in their games,
> The little boy we led.

The worshipers said little as they made their way to
their cars, and down the sidewalks to their homes.

I was a visitor there that morning, and had you ridden
home with me you might have heard me talking to
myself. If so, here's what you'd have heard:

"Of all the ministers I've known, this Preacher has
helped me most. I once thought a good Christian never
hurts inside, that with faith, you didn't suffer like other
folks. Then when the Preacher told us how he could
quote the poetry but heard no music to go with the
words, I began to identify with him. He helped me see
that only the suffering can help the sufferers. I guess all
of us need heroes; I know we all need fellow sufferers."

Heavenly Fire

During one of the worst thunderstorms of the summer, lightning struck the steeple of Tinyburg Church. Damage to the steeple was slight, but when the trustees examined the belfry, they discovered that some of the massive wood trusses which support the cast-iron bell had rotted out. "Too expensive to repair," they concluded, deciding instead to remove the bell and mount it on a concrete slab in the churchyard.

Even Uncle Billy "Told-You-So" Cutrell, who lives across the street, agreed. Still miffed that the church voted to elect deacons for three-year terms instead of for life, he offered his own opinion about the storm: "The fire of God on a stiff-necked people!"

As soon as the word spread, the Preacher got a call from Will Webb, president of Tinyburg Builders Supply. "Preacher," he began, "you folks can't tear down that steeple. You just can't. It's part of Tinyburg."

"I guess I've never told you," he continued, "but six or seven years ago, Mrs. Webb was seriously sick. One morning, just about daylight, after I'd set up with her all night, I looked out her hospital window. The first rays of the sun were striking the steeple of your church."

"Just then, a feeling welled up inside me that said, 'If your wife gets well, she'll need more help than she's

getting in this hospital.' Ordinarily, Preacher, I'm not a
praying man, but me and the Lord had a little talk, right
there. Late that afternoon, when the doctor came by, he
smiled, 'Will, the crisis is past.'"

"I'll never forget that sunrise against the steeple, and
that's why there's no way it's ever gonna come down."

When the Preacher explained their plight, Will interrupted. "Preacher, if some of your men can help, I'll
furnish the materials plus one or two of my employees.
We'll be over at sunup, Saturday morning. Get your
womenfolk to fry us a chicken dinner, and by sundown
you'll have a steeple and belfry as good as new."

And so it was. Even Uncle Billy sauntered across the
street by late afternoon and wielded a paint brush,
reaching what he could by standing on the ground.

Will Webb even attended services the next morning.
"Preacher, I'm not much of a sermon man," he explained
as he came in. "Never did get used to churchgoing, all
that standing up and sitting down, turn to this page and
that chapter, sing this verse, and quote that. But if a
steeple has anything to do with pointing a man to
heaven, I figure on finding the way!"

About that time Uncle Billy walked in, "Say, Will, this
is the first time I can remember seeing you in church."

And Will, winking at the Preacher, smiled, "Well,
Uncle Billy, I guess this is the first time the fire of God
ever fell on this congregation."

Uncle Billy's Birthday Party

On July 23, Uncle Billy "Told-You-So" Cutrell would be eighty years old. When Mrs. Clay Barker suggested they surprise him with an all-church birthday party, Aunt Sarah Biggs raised two big questions.

"In the first place, you can't surprise Uncle Billy, for he has a way of finding out everything that's going on," Aunt Sarah said. "And in the second place, Uncle Billy doesn't believe in eating in the church, and what's a party without refreshments?"

"If you'll make me chairman of the committee, I'll find a way to pull it off," Mrs. Barker volunteered. And so it was.

The event was announced in the church bulletin as a baby shower for an expectant mother in the young marrieds' class. It would be in the church basement at 7:30 PM on July 23. Only women were invited.

As for a gift, everyone agreed that a new suit would be the ideal choice. Since Uncle Billy's wife had died, he had grown a little careless in his dress. A slight, stooped fellow, he was not over 5' 4" and seldom weighed more than 120 pounds. In fact, he had always been hard to fit. Years ago, a salesman for Modern Men's Wear in Bigtown told him so.

"Mr. Cutrell, it's awfully hard to fit you," the clerk

155

complained. "You don't have much of a waist—that is, your hips don't hold up your trousers."

"I'm not dependin' on any hips to hold up my britches," Uncle Billy shot back. "That's why I wear these suspenders, and I've never lost a pair of pants in public yet!"

(Uncle Billy's broad, police-style suspenders were his trademark, and he was never without them. Like the two elastic garters he wore just above his elbows, to tuck in his shirt sleeves that always seemed too long, he wouldn't feel dressed without them).

After Uncle Billy had tried on just about every suit in the store, the clerk suggested, "Mr. Cutrell, I'm going to send you over to the boys' department; you'll be a lot happier with the feel and fit of the sizes they stock."

"Look here, Mister," Uncle Billy bristled. "You're not sending me nowhere. I'm a grown man, and you're not about to fit me with little boy stuff. And another thing. If you want my advice as to what you should wear, I suggest a pair of rompers—they'd match your personality!"

With that last remark, Uncle Billy realized he'd gone too far. But without apology, he walked out and, for twenty years, had never stepped foot in Modern Men's Wear.

Instead, he did all his shopping at the Tinyburg Dry Goods Store. "May not be as much choice," he explained to a neighbor one day, "but they don't insult you here in Tinyburg. And besides, they still carry one-piece long underwear and my brand of suspenders."

Knowing all of this, Mrs. Barker acted rather nonchalant when she stopped Uncle Billy after prayer meeting one night. "Uncle Billy, I've got a problem," she began. This immediately caught his ear, for Uncle Billy liked nothing better than to solve problems.

"You remember my grandson, Brad, who lives in New Jersey? Well, he's going to be sixteen next month. And I want to send him a nice, tailored suit.

"The tailor over at Modern Men's Wear is making it, but the problem's getting the right fit.

"I was wondering, since you're both about the same size, if you'd be willing to go over to Bigtown and let him take your measurements? Brad's not a boy anymore—you'd be surprised how he's grown. I just have a feeling that if we fit the suit to you, it will fit Brad almost perfectly."

Uncle Billy agreed, and Mrs. Barker drove him to Bigtown the next day. He seemed pleased to help and enjoyed the attention of the tailor who never once referred to his small waist and narrow hips.

"Come back in two weeks," the tailor said, "and I'll have it ready for you to try on."

Right on the day, two weeks later, Mrs. Barker and Uncle Billy drove back to Bigtown, stopping at Billy's favorite drive-in for lunch. "Mrs. Barker, you sure are nice to an old man," Uncle Billy said gratefully, wiping mustard off his mouth with his shirt sleeve.

The suit was a dark-grey, all-wool herringbone. "Mr. Cutrell, before you try this on, I want you to put on a dress shirt and tie, so we can see just how the suit's going to look on Brad. Go over to that stack of white, Oxford cloth, button-down shirts, and select your size. I already have a tie—this navy-and-wine stripe. And while you're at it, try on a pair of those black, wing-tip dress shoes, so we can better gauge the cuff length."

Uncle Billy had never felt so well-dressed in his life. "Hot diggity," he said, looking in the mirror. "Why, if I

wore an outfit like this next Sunday, every widow woman
in church would want to sit on my pew! Brad's sure going
to be proud. And the pants fit so snug, you don't even
need suspenders."

Back in the tiny dressing cubicle, Uncle Billy took one
final look at himself in the mirror. Cocking his head
jauntily, and with a sly wink, he concluded that it would
take *two* pews to hold all the widow women who would
like to sit with him! Then, with a pensive look, he ran his
fingers once more down the sharp creases of the new
trousers, before putting on his faded wash pants.

The night of the baby shower, Uncle Billy had already
pulled off his shoes as the first step in a lengthy bedtime
ritual when there was a knock at the door. It was Mrs.
Barker.

"Uncle Billy," she began, with an anxious tone. "All
the ladies were over in the church for the shower when
the lights went out. Must have blown a fuse. Do you have
any idea where the fuse box is?"

Since he lived right across the street, Uncle Billy was
used to lost keys, lights left burning, dogs locked in rest
rooms, and the like. "Let me put on my shoes and find
my flashlight, and I'll be right over," he promised.

Even though the basement was dark, Uncle Billy
thought he could make out an unbelievably large number
of persons, including men and children as well.

Then, just as he screwed in a new fuse and the lights
came on, he was almost deafened as more than a hundred
well-wishers began singing:

> **Happy birthday to you!**
> **Happy birthday to you!**
> **Happy birthday, Uncle Billy,**
> **Happy birthday to you!**

"Some baby shower . . . some burned-out fuse!" scolded Uncle Billy, good heartedly.

At this point Clay Barker, wearing both his diamond stickpin and six-diamond wedding band, plus his dozen fountain pens and ball-point pens in his breast pocket, took over as master of ceremonies.

"Uncle Billy, we apologize for keeping you up past your bedtime, but it's not every day we get to honor a nice fellow like you on his eightieth birthday," Clay began. "We don't have a lot of speeches. Instead, we're gonna' join in a sing-along and do a lot of make-believing tonite. So let's imagine we're all one big barbershop quartet. Lots of harmonizing—won't even bother with a piano."

And so they did, singing on and on into the summer night, while fireflies on the church lawn, as if caught up in the ecstasy of it all, seemed to swoop and dive and dance to the tempo of the music.

They started out with such numbers as:

> Jim crack corn I don't care,
> Jim crack corn I don't care,
> Jim crack corn I don't care,
> Ole Massa gone away.

Folk Song, Anonymous

> When Johnny Comes Marching Home Again,
> Hurrah, hurrah,
> We'll give him a hearty welcome then,
> Hurrah, hurrah;
> The men will cheer, the boys will shout
> The ladies they will all turn out,
> And we'll all feel gay,
> When Johnny Comes Marching Home.

PATRICK S. GILMORE

The sun shines bright in the old Kentucky home,
'Tis summer, the darkies are gay;
The corn top's ripe and the meadow's in the bloom,
While the birds make music all the day.

STEPHEN C. FOSTER

Then the tempo picked up as they sang "The Spanish Cavalier," "We Shall Not be Moved," "You Can't Get to Heaven on Roller Skates," and "Billy Boy."

Then followed "She'll Be Coming 'Round the Mountain," "Go Tell Aunt Rhody," "Old MacDonald," "Ezekiel Saw The Wheel," and "I've Been Workin' on the Railroad."

At this point, Uncle Billy interrupted, "How about all the menfolks serenading the ladies with some romancin' numbers?" And so they did:

I'll take you home again, Kathleen,
Across the ocean wild and wide,
To where your heart has ever been,
Since first you were my bonnie bride.

THOMAS P. ESTENDORF

Let me call you sweetheart,
I'm in love with you;
Let me hear you whisper
That you love me, too—
Keep the love light glowing
In your eyes so true;
Let me call you sweetheart,
I'm in love with you.

BETH SLATER WHITSON

By now, Uncle Billy had long since forgotten that it

was past bedtime. "I'm not the singer I used to be, but I was quite a boy soloist in my younger days," he announced next. "And I just thought of an old ballad that I often sang at our school pie suppers. And if you can bear with an eighty-year-old 'operatic tenor,' I'll sing it for you right now."

And so he did, swaying back and forth to the tempo, his eyes closed in reverie.

> Hand me down my walkin' cane,
> Hand me down my walkin' cane,
> O hand me down my walkin' cane,
> I'm gonna leave on the midnight train
> 'Cause all my sins are taken away,
>   taken away.
>
> Now if I die in Tennessee,
> Now if I die in Tennessee,
> Now if I die in Tennessee,
> Ship me back by C.O.D.,
> 'Cause all my sins are taken away,
>   taken away.

Everyone was nearly hoarse when Clay finally called a stop. "Sorry folks, but we've got lots more planned. Now we want Uncle Billy to come up here and open his present."

Uncle Billy had been eyeing the big package, done in fancy ribbon, and his curiosity had grown by the minute.

With trembling hands, he untied the ribbon and pulled back the gaily decorated paper. And there, in all its glory, was "Brad's new outfit"—the wool, dark-grey herringbone suit, the white, Oxford-cloth button-down shirt, the wine-and-navy striped tie, the wing-tip black shoes. Only now, his lips quivered, as well as his hands,

as he held up the suit for all to see.

"Speech! Speech! Speech!" everyone cried.

"I'm not a speech maker," Uncle Billy apologized. "About all I know to say is 'I told-you-so' when anyone gets in a scrape!"

"OK," replied Clay. "We'll let you off from the speech making. But let me toss you a question or two, that most folks were too polite to ask. How is it that you always seem to come up with the right answer?"

Uncle Billy thought for a minute, slowly fingering his new navy-and-wine-colored tie. "First, I want to thank you for these new clothes. I just hope Brad's not disappointed, and that his grandparents will use these measurements to order a suit for him. But I tell you folks, the first cool Sunday this fall, when I get all dressed up, the pew where I sit won't hold all the widows!"

Then, pointing to his white hair, he added, "As I've told you folks lots of time, there may be snow on the mountain, but there's still fire in the furnace!

"Now as to how I always come up with the right answer. 'Course that's an exaggeration. No one's right all the time. As you know, I don't have much formal education. Worked for years as a laborer with the Tinyburg street department, before I retired. But I always tried to profit by my mistakes. The times I said, 'I told you so,' wasn't because I was so smart—just that I'd been over the same road before, and never forgot the lesson. That's what I call wisdom.

"There's a verse in the Bible, Proverbs 2:4 I believe, that tells us to seek for wisdom like we'd hunt for silver or buried treasure.

"And Proverbs 4:18 is another verse which I've sort of taken as a motto. It reads, 'The path of the just is as the shining light, that shineth more and more unto the perfect day.'

"Oh, I don't mean every day's been bright. Like everybody else, I've had my share of disappointments. Things didn't always work out. There've been times when I was wrong, days when I was right."

As Uncle Billy finished, they broke into sustained applause, waking some of the toddlers who had fallen asleep in their parents' laps.

"And now for the refreshments!" beamed Clay, as he pointed to the long row of ice cream freezers which the folks had brought from home.

At this point, Uncle Billy shifted uneasily in his seat. He never felt right about serving meals and eating in the church. Yet he didn't want to be rude. His only concession had been Vacation Bible Schools.

"Those youngsters need something cool to refresh them on hot mornings," he always said. "And so long as we serve them outside, under the trees, I see no harm." In fact, for several years he'd volunteered to help serve the refreshments.

"And now for the refreshments," Clay continued. "Uncle Billy, I said earlier that we'd do a lot of play-liking tonight. So right now, let's play like it's Vacation Bible School time, and we're all going outside for refreshments."

Uncle Billy felt the tension relax in his clinched fists. *That Clay Barker's one smart cookie,* he said to himself, as he moved outside to the tables spread under a canopy of Japanese lanterns.

"So long as we're going to eat on the church grounds anyway," he said to Aunt Sarah, who was cutting the cake, "might as well give me that big, thick centerpiece with the maraschino cherries on top!"

After everyone had eaten twice as much as they needed, the honoree made one more request.

"Folks, I hate to see all this come to an end. As my daddy used to say when I was a boy, 'It's been too big a boo for a yearling!'

"But before we go, could we all join hands, turn out these lights, and sing one more number for old Uncle Billy?

"Then I'd like to be excused without any more ado, just to slip out in the shadows, across the street, to home . . . "

And so they did, standing there under the stars, singing softly:

> There are loved ones in the glory
>   Whose dear forms you often miss,
> When you close your earthly story
>   Will you join them in their bliss?
>
> Will the circle be unbroken
>   By and by, by and by?
> In a better home awaiting
>   In the sky, in the sky?

ADA R. HABERSHON

Epilogue

I hope you've enjoyed these little visits to Tinyburg. I still get over there, now and then, for a day or so. Always eat breakfast at the Tinyburg Cafe, where I picked up so many of the stories you've just read.

Also, I continue to subscribe to the *Tinyburg News*, that comes out on Fridays. Since it's a small weekly, not much space is given to earth-shaking news on the national level.

But I enjoy reading about the friends I've made in Tinyburg—births, marriages, deaths, and the like. Also, I keep a sharp eye for items about any scrapes that Clay Barker may get into down at the courthouse!

And yes, I continue to write more Tinyburg Tales. The fact is, anytime you're fortunate enough to find a community that's south of Pretense, you're bound to run into one fascinating story after another.

Who knows? Maybe there'll be a second volume called *More Tinyburg Tales* or *Tinyburg Revisited*. I hope so, at least.

Oh, one more thing. If you ever visit there yourself, stop in the Tinyburg Cafe and mention my name. It's good for a free slice of homemade coconut pie. The proprietor—who's always looking for new business—asked me to include this little notice. And so I have, even if I waited until the last line of the last page.